Power, passion, and politics collide in an Elemental World that is ruled by the ancients.

WATERLOCKED

'wa-ter-locked' **adjective** Definition: enclosed entirely, or almost entirely, by water

Example: What happens when the water vampire you've promised yourself to actually wants you to go through with the wedding? For Gemma Melcombe, her engagement to Terrance Ramsay was a political maneuver. For Terry, it's something entirely more. Rough waters may be ahead for these two headstrong lovers, but until they come to an agreement, Gemma will be waterlocked.

WATERLOCKED is a stand-alone novella in the Elemental World series.

"...steamy, heart melting romance."
I Read Indie Book Blog

WATERLOCKED:
An Elemental World Novella

ELIZABETH HUNTER

To my amazing readers:
This one is one hundred percent dedicated
to you.
Thanks.

PROLOGUE

Terrance Ramsay was married to an absolute bitch, and he couldn't have been happier about it.

"You!" She climbed over the edge of the luxury yacht, dripping wet, as she would have to be to escape the elaborately secured day chamber on his favorite sailing vessel.

"Good evening, Gem. There's some dry clothes in the stateroom if you want some." He sipped a brandy and glanced at the white nightgown that clung to her slim frame. He'd never preferred skinny women. When Terry had been human, skinny meant poor, and the last thing the son of a farmer wanted when he came to the city was a woman who looked hungry. No, he'd always preferred a woman with a bit to hold on to. A generous bosom and bottom were his preference.

But then, one couldn't always control who they fell in love with.

"I do not want dry clothes, Terrance." Her voice was clipped and precise. It was the voice she used on her underlings, and Terry ignored how it set his fangs on edge. "I wish to know where we are. I wish to know how I got here. And then I demand to go back to London."

He wouldn't grin. No, he wouldn't. Well, maybe a little. "Well, luv, you can piss in one hand and wish in the other and see which one fills up faster. We're on our

1

honeymoon. Relax. And if you don't want dry clothes, you could always oblige me and wear none at all."

It took a lot to get Gemma to make that face. He tried not to enjoy it too much. Her mouth was hanging open and her blue eyes were wide. Oh, she was angry, all right. The last time she'd made that face had been before they were engaged and he'd had the gall to chat up her maid when she was in the room. Gemma had turned him down countless times at that point, but apparently, she didn't share. Even dishes that she hadn't found a taste for yet. She'd clocked him and had the brass to complain she'd broken a nail. They were engaged two days later.

"After all," Terry continued, "you don't see me wearing any clothes." Her wide eyes finally flicked down to the loose towel he wore around his waist. He didn't care for swimming clothes. He was a water vampire. He was at home in his element and clothes weren't something he wore unless he was forced.

"I have a charity luncheon tomorrow!" She stamped her foot. It was adorable.

"I'd say I'm sorry, but I'm not. I'm sure Wilhelmina will make your excuses for you. That's why you pay her."

She hissed at him. "I need to go back to London. I don't know what mad scheme this is, but I'm not a fan of your pranks. I have responsibilities, people depending on me. And if you think you can—"

"We're alone, Gem. Middle of the ocean with no land in sight. I'm almost as powerful as you are out here. Imagine that. No maids. No chefs. No minions scurrying about to tend to your every whim. Also, no meetings. No luncheons. No responsibilities other than the one to relax and indulge the imagination of your new husband."

She was seething. "Indulge the imagination of—"

"No need to be proper here." He grinned and let his fangs run out, deliberately looking her up and down like the choice morsel she was. No, he'd never cared for skinny women in the past, but then, Gemma wasn't precisely skinny. She was just slim. She had a fine waist with a nice curve to her ass. Her breasts... well, he'd become rather fond of those, even if they were on the small side. Even more fond of her reaction when he paid them proper attention. And if he wasn't mistaken, they rather liked his attention at the moment, despite what their mistress might protest.

Oh, he was going to get it for that, especially when he let her see the full effect of his lazy perusal. He threw off the towel, stretched his arms behind his head, and lay back for her examination. "Get rid of the clothes, luv."

She couldn't stop her eyes from traveling over him. Never had been able to, not from the first night they'd met over a hundred years before. Part of her hated him for it. He may have been handsome, but he was a bruiser and a cad. There wasn't a proper bone in Terry's body and his manners were rough to say the least. Terrance Ramsay was the last man in the world that Gemma Melcombe thought she should want for eternity.

And Terry knew he was the only man in the world she needed.

She tried to roll her eyes at him. "Stop showing off. Put some clothes on and take me back to England."

He stood slowly and walked toward her, naked and aroused by anger and desire. The moon was almost full and it made her blond hair shine silver. She was a vision. They were in the middle of the Atlantic, not a bit of land in sight, with no lights other than the stars, and she stood long, slim, and furious with the water shining on her skin. God help him. He was completely at her mercy, no matter what element surrounded them, but he'd be damned if he let her see it.

Her delicate chin jutted out when he approached. Her blue eyes narrowed when he lifted his hands. Then widened when he took the straps of her nightgown in his fingers, tore the thing right down the center, and tossed it over the side of the boat.

Terry grinned when he glanced down. "There. Much better."

Gemma screamed and leapt on him, knocking him to his back and punching his jaw when his head hit the deck. If he'd had to breathe, he would have been in trouble.

"I hate you!" She punched him again before he had both her wrists in his grasp. When she couldn't free them, she leaned down and head-butted him. "Take me home!"

"Lord, you're a good fighter," he grunted. "Knew I married you for a reason."

"Take me back!" she yelled, wrenching one arm around to pin his neck to the deck.

"No." His voice was hoarse, but it wasn't as if he was really hurting for air. Still, it was uncomfortable.

"I hate you!"

"You said that already."

"First—" She dug her nails in his neck, drawing blood. "—you trick me into that sham of a wedding. Then, you kidnap me and bring me out here to the middle of nowhere—"

"Enough!" He bared his teeth, finally losing patience with her. Terry had been right. On land, she was far, far more powerful than he was. He liked it. Liked being the partner of a woman who others feared. It had always been part of her appeal to him. But on the water? They were equals. That was part of the plan. He rolled her over and pinned her to the teak deck, grabbing her hands and pushing them up over her head as his thighs locked around her waist. They were both naked, the unmistakably erotic position did little to quell his desire, but what she'd said...

"...that sham of a wedding..."

He leaned down and hissed in her ear, "Say what you want, Gemma. Curse me and punch me if you will. I know you're spitting mad, and that's fine. But do not lie. There was nothing about our wedding that was a sham."

She turned her head to meet his eyes. "Bullshit. You promised to lo—"

Terry leaned down and stopped her mouth with a furious kiss. Then he pulled back a fraction of an inch and whispered, "Nothing was a sham."

Gemma looked up at him in frank shock, no doubt remembering the vows he'd spoken. Vows he spoke before God and their clans. She knew, better than anyone else, that Terry didn't make promises he didn't keep. He slid sensuously down her body and kissed her open mouth again, flicking her tongue with his own, teasing the inside of her mouth as his amnis reached out to follow the drops of water that still covered her skin. Feeling the rush of energy, she gave a completely involuntary moan of pleasure.

His thighs pressed around her, but his hands

loosened their grip on her wrists. His fingers dove into the wet strands of her hair, twisting them as he pulled her closer. And the desire that bound them—the desire she fought and bucked against—pulled them both closer. Her amnis, the electrical current that hummed under her skin and animated her immortal life, reached toward his, wrapping around him and causing his skin to throb in response.

Her power utterly floored him.

With a surge, she rolled Terry over so she was the one pinning him down. She pulled her lips from his and looked on in triumph, but Terry kept his expression carefully blank. She couldn't know. Couldn't. He'd lose any advantage he ever had. If Gemma knew how madly he was in love with her, she could destroy him.

She threw her head back and the wet hair slapped against her skin. "Concede?"

"No."

She didn't look surprised, only annoyed.

He stretched his arms up again and knit his fingers together behind his head, flexing the muscles in his arms and chest. Gemma looked down again.

"Forget what you were sitting on, luv?"

"Cocky."

"You'd know." He thrust his hips up and arched an eyebrow at her. "Might as well put it to good use, wife. We'll be here until I say we can leave."

CHAPTER ONE

Two weeks earlier...

The night sped past, shocks of light slashing through the backseat of the black sedan Terry's driver maneuvered through the twisting streets of the city. He'd lived in London for over two hundred years, but he still loved it. He loved the pulse and life of it. The dirty corners and the ragged edges where the street collided with the more refined elegance of what London had become. The city reeked of money some nights, the same way that it had stunk of garbage and coal one hundred years before.

Terry liked money. Money and power. Money, power, and the occasional bright spot of beauty that reminded him it was all worth it. Was he a good man? He lifted a finger to tap on the glass, ticking a staccato rhythm against the lights as they drove. A smile curled the corner of his mouth.

Good was highly subjective.

"The Spanish delegation will be here tomorrow evening, Mr. Ramsay." The sound of his human secretary's voice cut through his ruminations.

"How many?"

"Five. One of Leonor's lieutenants and four others."

"No introduction?"

"None that they've requested."

"Hmm." So it would be someone Terry had met before. Five vampires from Spain. Who would his old associate send? Raul? Melinda, maybe? It all depended on what she wanted and how hard she was willing to tug on their tenuous connection. A connection that had mostly been formed by Gemma's machinations, if the truth were told.

"I've called the office and they've already arranged a conference room with some donors available. We'll have a selection of cocktails before the meeting, as well as some—"

"I want them at the house, Carl."

His secretary looked confused for a moment. "Excuse me? The house?"

"And call Wilhelmina. Clear it with her, but I want Gemma there. Have her rearrange her schedule if it doesn't fit." The Spaniards wouldn't be expecting the house in Mayfair, and he wanted his fiancé's read on the situation. She knew Leonor better than Terry did.

Poor Carl was still floundering, no doubt dreading the thought of telling Gemma's secretary her employer's schedule might have to be preempted for a business meeting. "I'm sorry, Mr. Ramsay, but could you please explain—"

Terry cut him off with a single raised finger. He turned to his first lieutenant, Roger, and spoke in a lower voice. "Send the boys out tonight. Find out who's coming, then call Gemma. Take the proper steps."

"Yes, boss."

He turned back to the thin man in the respectable suit. "Carl, brief the office about the change of venue. I

8

have a feeling this is about something other than the trade deal she talked about."

"Sir, this meeting has been planned for months. It's a routine—"

"Trade would be three. She's sending five."

"Yes, Mr. Ramsay."

"And Roger, have Wilson and Kincaid at dinner."

He saw Roger crack a smile. "Kincaid?"

"He'll behave if Gemma's there."

Roger murmured, "I suppose we'll finally see if those etiquette lessons paid off."

"As long as he eats with a fork, it'll be an improvement."

Carl picked up again, rattling off more matters Terry tucked to the back of his brain to think about later. Five vampires from Spain? This week had suddenly become far more interesting.

Terry picked up the foreign scent as soon as he stepped out of the car in Mayfair. It was hardly past two in the morning, but he'd finished his duties early that night and had anticipated a quiet evening at home. Perhaps he'd even convince Gemma to sit still long enough to talk about something more than work. But if he was there...

"Oy." He slammed the front door closed, cutting off Roger, who had tried to slip into the house behind him. "What are you doing here?" Terry shouted as he walked down the hall. Daniel Rathmore was already sitting in Terry's favorite chair in the study, sipping a Scotch in a cut crystal glass, the surrounding elegance seemingly at ease with the young vampire's scruffy appearance.

"This is an excellent whisky."

"It should be for what I paid for it. Out of my chair. No respect from the in-laws, eh?"

Daniel gave him a sly grin as he hopped up and bowed in mock ceremony. "Daniel Rathmore, son of Carwyn ap Bryn, brother of Gemma Melcombe, asks your favor in visiting the City of London, Mr. Ramsay."

Terry gave Daniel's cheek a quick slap and grabbed his glass. "Mr. Rathmore would be far more welcome if he'd wait till I got home to begin pouring my drink. How are you, lad? And where've you been? She's been asking about you." He took a sip of Scotch and sat in the newly vacated chair. "Almost had your sister worried, Dan. Don't irritate me like that."

Daniel had the grace to feign embarrassment. "Mountain climbing. Didn't think to call. It's the best season in South America. And there was a woman."

"Isn't there always with you?" He took another sip. It really was an excellent bottle. "South America, eh?"

Daniel was about to say something else when they both turned. Gemma's powerful amnis announced her presence even before her scent did. Then the smell of her blood hit Terry, and he felt the instant tension. His fangs lengthened. His trousers grew tight as his amnis swirled around him, aching to stroke along hers. He felt the blood begin to pump in his veins as she entered the room. It had always been like this for him, from the moment he'd laid eyes on her. He was long past being annoyed by it.

"Daniel!" Gemma was a vision of elegance in a designer suit and perfectly appropriate jewelry. Jewelry she'd picked out herself. Smelling of a very light perfume she'd also picked out. "Where have you been, darling? I was almost ready to send out a search party." She walked over and gave Terry a perfunctory kiss on the cheek before she headed to her brother.

Gemma was the oldest of her siblings now, and Daniel was the youngest. Carwyn claimed he was finished siring children, but who knew what would happen with a new young wife. Gemma had only one child, a young vampire who lived in Sydney. They rarely spoke, but corresponded regularly. It was Daniel, the youngest of their clan, she doted on.

"I'm fine, Gem." The two embraced, Gemma caring not a mite for her brother's scruffy appearance. "And I was in Cochamó. Gus and Isa say hello. Want to know when you two are coming for a visit."

Gemma gave a mock shudder. "And travel that long on a boat? No thank you. Maybe if Giovanni sent the plane. Far more civilized way to travel."

Terry felt the fang pierce the inside of his lip as his jaw clenched. Wait for it...

"Was he there?" She asked so nonchalantly. "With... the family? It's such a lovely time of the year to visit."

Terry took another sip of whisky and buried the snarl.

Fucking Italian.

"No, I think they're all in California right now. The valley was nice and deserted. Gus and I were climbing in this new area, Gemma. It was so beautiful."

They chattered for another twenty minutes about Daniel's latest adventure. Gemma laughed—really laughed—as her brother regaled her with wild stories and jokes about their kin in the New World. Terry poured drinks for all of them and slipped out for a moment to take a drink from one of the house donors, then he answered a call from Roger, who had already found out who the Spanish delegate would be and what his favorite wine was.

He walked back in the library just as his brother-in-law was finishing a story.

"—always seems so proper. If I hadn't seen it myself, I'd never believe it. But then, you'd know all about that."

Gemma gave him a slightly guilty glance before her eyes darted away, and Daniel's laughter trailed off.

Who could you have been talking about, darling? I just can't imagine...

Daniel smiled at Terry. "All finished with work, then?"

"For now. How long are you staying, Dan?"

"Just a week or so. I really need to get back to the house. I'm sure the sheep miss me." Daniel—well, Daniel's day man—ran a small organic farm that catered to high-end restaurants in Southwest England and Wales. He'd recently begun making cheese. Terry shook his head at the thought. Ridiculous occupation for a vampire, in his opinion, but it made the young man happy and left him enough time and money to roam the world whenever he liked, which was really all Daniel cared about.

Plus, it was fairly good cheese.

"You'll stay with us, then." Gemma grabbed his hand in a squeeze. "I'll have your room prepared."

"Already done, Gem. And you might want to speak to Wilhelmina. There's a few changes to the schedule for tomorrow night. Dinner party."

WATERLOCKED

Her eyes tightened in disapproval. "I have a meeting with the mayor's people tomorrow night."

"You'll have to reschedule." He flicked a glance at Daniel, then looked back into her eyes. "This is a priority."

She wanted to argue with him, but wouldn't in front of her brother. And that was only one of the reasons that Terry was marrying her. Gemma knew the value of a united front. They might have fought like cats and dogs behind closed doors, but in front of anyone else, they were ever in agreement.

Still, her eyes were frosty when she said, "I'll speak to Mina. I'm sure something can be arranged."

"She has all the details. So does Carl."

With a regal nod, she stood. "Danny, I imagine you want to clean up before dawn. You know where everything is. Make yourself at home, of course." She didn't spare him a glance when she walked out of the room.

Daniel waited until the hall was silent before he snickered. "You'll hear it later, mate."

Terry shrugged. "I always do. How many times did she ask about the bloody Italian?"

Daniel paused, watching as Terry poured another whisky. "She didn't ask—"

"Yes, she did."

"Not directly."

Terry humored the man with a lazy smile. "She's too smart for that."

"She's not in love with him. Not really."

At that, Terry let out a hearty laugh. "Oh really?"

"She's in love with the *idea* of him. He's cultured,

13

sophisticated. Values education and music and all those things Gemma thinks she needs to be happy."

Terry handed Daniel another drink and clinked his glass. "Cheers. In other words, he's the complete opposite of me."

Daniel continued as if Terry hadn't spoken. "Which is ridiculous, of course. You're exactly the kind of man she needs. You're not too polite to call her on her bullshit, and you're smart enough for her. She respects you, Terry."

She respected Giovanni Vecchio, too. Hell, Terry respected Vecchio; the man was a formidable ally and he certainly never encouraged Gemma's attentions. Well, not in the last hundred years or so. Terry cleared his throat. "Aye. We'll make a very good partnership, Gem and me. Good for us both. Good for London, too."

Daniel grinned. "So pragmatic, Mr. Ramsay. You're in love with her, aren't you? How terribly inconvenient."

Terry said nothing, flicking his tongue over a long fang as Daniel watched him with an amused expression.

"Well, you'll just have to convince her to be in love with you, too. You've certainly never lacked chemistry. That much is obvious."

Terry had to smile. "Chemistry, my boy, has never been the problem."

"Then what?"

If he knew the answer to that, Terry wouldn't be chatting with the annoying earth vampire in his study, would he? Once again, Daniel plowed on, obviously amused with his older sister's romantic entanglements. "How long have you been engaged now?"

"Ten years."

The boy almost looked offended. "Why on earth so long?"

Terry shrugged. "Never pressed the issue. She's here, ain't she? She's mine. I'm hers. Ten years isn't that long in the grand scheme of things. You have to remember, she's a bit older than the two of us."

"Still, high time you two wed, in my opinion." Daniel nodded firmly. "That'll nail her down, then you can work on the love bit."

Terry shook his head. "How do you get as many women as you do, Dan?"

"Stunning good looks." It was true. The young man had been turned in his early twenties and had a roguish beauty that women fawned over. "In fact, you should marry this week! While I'm here. Use it for leverage. I'd absolutely hate to miss my favorite sister's wedding, and I'm always jaunting off on wild adventures. You just never know when I'll be around."

He cocked an eyebrow. Now that idea had potential. "I suppose I could speak to a judge I know—"

"No! What are you thinking?" Daniel's eyes widened. "A church wedding, you daft man. Or at least a proper man of the cloth. She'll renege on a civil arrangement the minute things don't suit her. But a church wedding..."

Terry scoffed. "Gemma's never been devout."

"Ah..." Daniel slid forward with a glint in his eye. "But she is our father's daughter. Trust me, if you want her to stick around, a church wedding is a must, my friend."

Terry narrowed his eyes. "Why are you telling me this? What do you have to gain?"

The teasing glint left his eyes and Daniel smiled

sincerely. "The happiness of my favorite sister, Ramsay. Because, I think you're good for her. And honestly? She's half in love with you already, she just doesn't realize it."

"Thank you so much, gentlemen. What a pleasure it was to see you all." Gemma graciously saw their guests to the door the next night. "And Guillermo, please tell Leonor I'm looking forward to seeing her on our next holiday."

"Of course, Señora." The Spaniard bent over her hand. "It would be my honor."

"You're too kind."

"Your hospitality honors me and my patroness."

Gemma batted her lashes at the handsome man, who had made every effort to charm the leading woman of London immortal society all night. He'd simpered and flirted, shooting Gemma deep, meaningful looks every time Terry opened his mouth or one of the guards did something he interpreted as vulgar.

'How tolerant you are,' his dark eyes said, *'to put up with such loutish behavior.'*

Terry didn't know why the Spaniard was complaining. Kincaid had only fumbled the silverware once. If it happened to be a steak knife through one of the Spanish guards' hands... well, accidents did happen.

Gemma was wearing a slim burgundy suit that hugged her ass and showed off her trim waist and figure. She wasn't a tall woman. In fact, she was delicate-looking, if you didn't know better. And she was stunning. Gemma had classic features that were beautiful no matter what the current fashion was. He'd caught more than one of their guests giving her the eye before they caught Terry's possessive glare.

He watched her with a predatory stare as she made all the polite noises necessary to make their guests leave. He was leaning against the wall leading to their basement chambers as Gemma conferred a few moments with her assistant, then with the housekeeper. Terry muttered the usual goodnights to Carl and Roger before he managed to pull her through the door and secure it so they were truly alone.

She let out a deep breath, crossing her arms and biting her lip thoughtfully. "This is not good. Did you notice how many times Guillermo mentioned the Portuguese coast? What's going on there?"

"Don't give a shit at the moment." He strode toward her as her mouth dropped open in protest.

"Terry, this is impor—"

He cut her off as he pulled her in for a possessive kiss, branding her mouth with his. He reached down and grabbed a handful of her backside, bringing her up hard against him as he spun them around. He guided her backward down the steps. She gave only one muffled protest before her nails were digging into his shoulders and ripping away the silk tie she'd forced him to wear.

Terry lifted his head, grinning around his fangs. Political machinations always stirred her blood.

"You were brilliant," he said as he tugged at the buttons on her jacket. "Fucking brilliant as always, Gem."

"Of course I was. Mmm..." She kissed him again, nipping at his lips. Not enough to draw blood though. Oh no, they were quite careful about that, weren't they? "Kincaid couldn't have timed that knife better. You were about to explode."

Damn buttons. There were too many of them on her shirt. "If that bloody Spaniard had batted his fucking lashes at you one more time—"

"I was playing with him, Terry." She lost patience and ripped his shirt down the middle when they were half-way down the stairs. "Don't you like to see me toy with my prey?" She reached down and cupped him in his trousers, stroking through the tailored wool as he groaned.

"You can play with that any time you like, luv."

She gave a throaty chuckle and licked up the center of his chest. Damn her silk shirt. He took it by the collar and tore it away. Then he reached down to the slit at the back of her skirt and rid her of the bottom half, too.

"I liked that suit." She crossed her arms, pouting as she stood in nothing more than a set of frilly lingerie at the foot of the stairs.

"So did the Spaniards. I'll buy you another."

He picked her up as if she weighed nothing, taking her to his room at the far end of the basement where he threw her on the bed before he went back to secure the door. Turning around, he could see that Gemma had already stripped off the last of her lingerie. Terry flicked the tip of his fang and smiled. She always had been admirably efficient.

"Now," she purred, "where were we? Oh yes, we were talking about the Portuguese coast—and what is probably a smuggling problem—while you got rid of those pants."

Terry slid the belt from his waist as he slowly walked toward her. "You're the one who picked out this suit.

Don't you like it?"

"Not at the moment." She leaned back in the pillows, stretching her arms over her head and arching her breasts up. He hissed and quickly rid himself of his pants, socks, and shoes before he crawled over her.

He started at the back of her knee, trailing his tongue up and over the inside of her thigh as he whispered, "Smuggling, eh?"

Gemma let out a slow breath. "It's been a problem for years. But it's gotten worse in the last six months or so, from what I've been able to find out."

He bent down, flicking his tongue for a quick taste before he continued up the crease of her thigh, circling her navel as he murmured, "Then why hasn't she come to us before? Leonor knows we have shared interest along that coast."

She grasped his head as he bent to lick first one breast, then the other. "No woman wants to appear weak. Certainly, not to her allies or those under her aegis."

Terry reached down, positioning himself at her center as he kissed her and drove in with one hard stroke. "Is that so?" He held still for a moment, until the haze cleared from her eyes and she wrapped her legs around his waist.

"Yes," she moaned. "That's so."

He began a slow, steady rhythm, a maddening one he knew would drive her out of her mind. Whatever problems his heart faced, in his bed, Terry had always known how to master her. He was an ardent pupil of Gemma's pleasure, an expert at reading her body, even if he couldn't read her mind. He locked his eyes with hers as she tried to push him to move faster.

Terry smothered a smile. It was a night for scheming, and he had plans of his own.

"Gemma, luv?"

"Yes!" She clutched at his neck, arching closer as he lifted the small of her back to change the angle.

"It seems as if our lives are about to get more complicated."

"I... agree. There, right there."

"Is that so?" He slowed and bent down to kiss along her collarbone as she gave a tortured moan. "It seems like it might be best to get a few things taken care of then. Before things get... distracting." He circled his hips in a practiced motion he knew she loved. Particularly when he was slow.

"Take care of... things. Yes. Good idea." Her tension was building again; he could feel it in every nerve as she clutched him closer.

Terry let his mind drift to the pure pleasure of their joining. The one place they had always made sense. Maybe it wasn't clear to her, but Terry knew with every drop of his immortal blood. Gemma Melcombe was the love of his life, the only woman he had ever wanted with this kind of fierce desire. And he didn't just love her, he needed her. More, he needed her to love him back. He wanted it with the same burning ambition that had caused him to seize power when others hesitated.

And Terrance Ramsay got what he wanted.

"Gemma," he groaned, forcing himself to slow again.

"What?" She ground her hips into his and dug angry fingers into his biceps.

He pressed his body down until they lay, skin to

skin. His hands framed her face and he stared into her eyes as he thrust slowly. They moved in sync, and the water in the room drew to his skin. His amnis caressed hers, twining around her limbs.

"Marry me, Gemma."

"Yes," she said. "I've already said yes."

He could see tears in the corners of her eyes, the pleasure held at bay for too many torturous minutes.

"Next week?"

She blinked rapidly. "What?"

He ground into her and his hand tangled in the hair at the nape of her neck. She cried out in surprise as he captured her lips again, swallowing the groan that wanted to escape his lips. "Marry me next week. I'm tired of waiting." *And so are you, my love.*

"Next week?" He could see her trying to object, so he pushed up and drove into her with another hard stoke. Her back arched in pleasure as she cried out.

"Yes. Next week." Sweet lord, he was about to explode. He clenched his jaw, keeping his eyes locked on her face. There it was. The hitch in her throat. The quiet gasping breath. He could hear the rush of the blood in her veins. "Yes, Gemma?"

"Yes." She let out a harsh breath as the tension drove her to the edge.

"Yes?" He wasn't quite sure what he was asking at that point, but a 'yes' from Gemma in his bed was never a bad thing.

Her eyes rolled back. "Yes!"

"Oh yes." His hips thrust one more time as he felt her climax with a spectacular scream. It shattered the last of his control, and he let himself come with a shout, closing his eyes and letting the amnis spark around their bodies. He slowed, then bent down to whisper a kiss across her mouth. It was slack with pleasure as he rolled to the side and curled his body around hers, trailing his lips along her shoulders, which were damp with water from his power. Finally, hidden from her keen eyes, he let himself grin.

Gotcha.

CHAPTER TWO

"Gemma, the plans for the new shelter need approval from the architectural firm."

She nodded at her assistant, still paging through the proposal from the charity in Birmingham that was petitioning for funds. "Put them on my desk, Mina. Then call Carl. He had some questions about security matters for the... wedding."

"Of course." She pretended not to notice the satisfied smile on Wilhelmina's face. She'd employed the woman for almost thirty years and had utter and complete faith in her professionally. She was also probably the closest thing that Gemma had to a friend. Her sisters, Deirdre and Isabel—as close as they were—did not count. "Have you finished your shopping? How about your dress?"

"The designer brought the finalized design to the house the other night. The fitting went well." At least she assumed that it did. The designer had cooed over the cut and drape of the satin, not complaining once about the rush of the order. Gemma had not even looked into the mirror. She hired the designer she normally used for her professional wardrobe. As a rule, he did not coo. Like others she employed regularly, she appreciated his professionalism and had come to trust him. If he said she looked stunning, she did.

"Any last minute details I can help with before the

weekend? The officiant? Has that been sorted out?"

"Terry is taking care of it. He has some human acquaintance who can take care of the legal matters."

"Ah. He must have been planning this for some time, then."

"Mina, you really ought to try to keep the smug tone from your voice. It's distracting."

"I'll try, dear, but it's hard when you've been proven right."

Gemma tried not to roll her eyes. It was an annoying habit she endeavored to avoid. Her assistant had told her only months before that her long-time fiancee had seemed... restless. Gemma thought he'd probably try to have an affair, which disappointed her on a level she didn't want to examine too closely. After all, she liked Terry. Maiming him and leaving London were hardly options she relished.

Wilhelmina, on the other hand, suggested that the foolish vampire had truly wanted to wed her. Ridiculous.

And apparently correct.

"So, you never did tell me how he managed to convince you down the aisle."

And I never will. "We had a conversation. He expressed his wishes. I expressed mine. We came to an agreement." *And a rather fabulous climax.*

Gemma tried not to curl her lip. She was still irritated with him. She'd been angry at first, so angry she didn't even linger in his rooms once the orgasmic haze had worn off. She hadn't yelled, either. She didn't need to. Terry knew how furious she was. They never slept together during the day, but she usually indulged in a brief respite of chatting and a second go, if things between them were pleasant. That night, she'd stormed out of his bedroom and hadn't touched him since.

She couldn't. Touching Terry was her weakness. It always had been.

"Well, everyone I speak to is excited about it. If nothing else, it'll be a fantastic party."

"It certainly will be." Gemma flipped through the estimate from the florist. By God, this wedding was going to cost a fortune, but they couldn't avoid it. In their position, they had to make a statement, and the union of one of the oldest clans in Britain with the young vampire leader of London was the event of the decade. Planning events had never been a problem for Gemma, but dealing with the particular needs of some of Britain's most... unusual citizens would have given her a headache if it was physically possible.

"Who knew it was so difficult to find lightly scented flowers this time of year?" The florist was shipping most of their stock in from hothouses in the Netherlands. That was only one of the special accommodations Gemma had to make. Delicately spiced food for sensitive taste buds. A string ensemble would take care of the task to not offend any preternaturally acute hearing. The aforementioned flowers...

All in less than a week. Bloody irritating water vampire.

She clipped through two more piles of messages, one having to do solely with the wedding, the other with the myriad business interests, charitable foundations, and family obligations that Gemma handled. It was less since Carwyn and Deirdre were splitting the load, but it still seemed like one of their clan or their extensive progeny was always in need of something. At the bottom of the family pile, there was a note written in a distinctive gaudy red ink.

'Can't wait for Friday night, luv.' —T

Gemma couldn't quite stifle the small snarl that erupted.

Daniel propped his hand on his chin, looking at her indulgently. "I just don't understand why you're so irritated, Gem. You'd agreed to marry the man anyway. You've been engaged for ten years now."

"Exactly." She sipped her pint and relaxed into the quiet corner booth at the pub where Daniel had dragged her. She was wearing denim pants and a snug t-shirt. Her regular heels had been replaced with a pair of casual boots. Only for Daniel. "There was nothing wrong with our relationship, in my opinion. Why on earth he had to go and complicate that by actually getting married is beyond me."

Daniel threw his head back and laughed. "You're such a control freak, Gemma."

"And that's why I've remained alive for as long as I have."

It was something she worried about with her brother. He had the same joyous disposition as their sire, but little of the wisdom or caution. Daniel was reckless.

Daniel winked. "Besides, isn't it time you married and settled down, old girl?"

"You're just asking for a beating. And what makes you think I haven't already?" She took a longer drink of the dark ale.

"What, married?" Daniel blinked in surprise. "You

were married?"

Gemma shrugged. "It was a long time ago."

"Well?" Daniel leaned closer and grinned. "What happened? You kill him when you got tired of him?"

She couldn't stop the instant rush of pain. Heartache. Regret. Even after so many hundreds of years. Daniel must have seen something in her eyes, because he pulled her a bit closer. "Gemma?"

"I don't like talking about it," she said.

"Please tell me. I can tell it bothers you, and knowing you, you've kept it to yourself. Does Father know?"

She gave a stiff nod. "Father and Ioan. They knew. It... it was a long time ago."

"Well?"

A laugh roared from the bar as a group of men heard the punchline of a joke. Laughter. It seemed like William had always laughed when he spoke her name. At least he had at first. "He was human. Didn't want to turn. We married anyway. We were married for fifteen years."

"He died?"

"Yes. There was an accident. We were out riding at night. I'd asked him to come. He fell off his horse. He was a good rider, but at night—" She broke off. "There was no one else there. His neck was broken, and I couldn't... I couldn't let him go."

Her brother let out a low breath, knowing exactly what had happened. The moment Gemma had saved William's life and turned her lover, the unique blood magic that tied them as sire and child had ravaged their feelings as husband and wife. Gemma would never forget it. She was weeping bloody tears when her husband had woken that first night. Ioan had been there, trying to comfort her, but nothing could. Everything about the man she had loved—had adored—had been utterly destroyed. William was still himself, but he could not look at her without shame. He had met the morning sun within months.

"I don't like talking about it," she said in a low voice. "That is the only time I married. I didn't need to follow the ridiculous customs of humans after that. I took whatever lovers I chose."

"You loved him. Your husband."

She cleared her throat. "Deeply. But I don't love Terry, so that's a relief."

"Gem—"

"Young." She turned and placed a hand on his cheek. "You are so young. Do you know how old I am, Daniel?"

"No. Younger than Ioan was."

"And older than Deirdre. We'll leave it at that. I do not fear solitude or the shifting tides of power. I take care of myself and those I am responsible for. My family, most of all. Marrying Terry is a good decision for me and our family."

"You should not marry for that reason." Poor Daniel looked as if he had tears in his eyes.

Gemma tried to comfort him. "I thought once there was someone I could love again, but he was not for me. I tried, Daniel. Terrance Ramsay is a wise choice."

"Wise?" he scoffed. "What of love? Passion? Romance? A mate to spend eternity—"

"Marriage and mating are two very different things. You should know that by now."

As often and as intense as their lovemaking was, Gemma had never offered her blood to Terry and he had never offered his to her. To offer and accept would bind them far more permanently than any trifling legal terms the humans set.

He sighed. "I just want you to be happy."

"And I am." She smiled. "I'm very pleased with Terry, even though he's irritating me at the moment. And if, in a hundred years I feel differently, then we'll go our separate ways. That's the benefit of marrying someone for practical reasons, Daniel."

"Isn't marriage supposed to be for the rest of your life?"

Gemma almost snorted. "We're not marrying in the church. This is a civil arrangement, that's all." Still, the thought of speaking vows—even civil ones—caused her stomach to clench. Then she pictured Terry saying them back and took a longer drink, ignoring the rush of blood that suddenly churned her veins.

She straightened the lace along the collar, stubbornly refusing to look into her reflection in the full-length mirror behind her.

"You look stunning, Gemma." Deirdre stood behind her, smiling wistfully. "I'm happy for you."

"Don't, Deirdre. It's not the same."

"You care for him, I can tell."

"Of course I do. He's an excellent companion. Trustworthy. Smart—"

"Yes, trustworthy and smart were exactly what your eyes were saying last night at dinner. You looked like you wanted to tear him to pieces or have him on the Chippendale buffet. I couldn't decide which."

"Neither could I." Did she say that out loud? She was

distracted. She usually indulged in Terry's very ardent attentions every other night or so, but since he'd wrangled the marriage promise out of her as he had, she'd been avoiding him. Idiotic, infuriating, stubborn, attractive, mouth-watering... why was she mad at him?

Gemma caught a glimpse of cream satin in the mirror. Wedding. Right.

Deirdre and Wilhelmina fussed with her simple dress. She hadn't wanted a veil or bustle. She'd lived when both were necessities of society and she found the fashions irritating and borderline insulting. No one would walk her down the aisle. In fact, she and Terry were walking in together. Equals in every way. Partners.

It was a marriage of practicality. An alliance of shared interests. Nothing more. She had no reason to feel nerves.

His mouth at her breast, worshiping her body as she writhed in pleasure.

She batted back the stylist who was hovering over her hair.

His arms braced over her, moving in that hard, steady rhythm.

At the last minute, she decided she didn't want to carry a bouquet. She left it dangling in Deirdre's hands.

His eyes as they focused on her, darkening as the tension built. Closer. Closer...

Rising, Gemma went to the door and opened it. At the end of the hall, she saw him. Dashing and deadly at the same time, Terry was clad in a elegantly tailored jacket that encased his muscular frame, but did not hide it. He locked eyes on her with the focus of a predator. She would have no courtly lover. No deferential husband. Here was a man she would fight with and fight alongside for the rest—

For as long as she found him agreeable. That was all.

Terry walked toward her slowly in the lavish hotel suite. Their friends and family were gathered in the ballroom downstairs. "Gemma."

"Terry."

He never took his eyes off her as he held out his hand.

Why was Gemma so worried? This was a partnership of two like-minded individuals, nothing more. She took his hand, ignoring the slow melt of desire she felt as his touch reminded her: This was why she had to avoid him. It was also why it was so hard to keep away. She could lie to others with ease, but she couldn't lie to herself. Terry was the finest, fiercest lover she'd ever had, and she wanted him with a desperate kind of desire that infuriated her. Even as they walked down the stairs, his thumb traced along the delicate vein at her wrist, causing her blood to pulse.

"I've been missing you, luv."

"Lots to do with the wedding details."

"Of course."

He knew she was lying.

"Are Carwyn and Brigid here?" she asked.

"And Deirdre. Daniel, of course. Your brother from France. Max and Cathy. Even Tavish came."

"Don't tell me he's wearing a tuxedo. That might give me nightmares."

He gave her a low chuckle and winked as they turned the corner. She could do this. It was just a party. A friendly party where she would have to sign a few papers and that would be—

She halted when the doors open and she saw the man in vestments standing at the front of the room.

"Terry," she hissed between a forced smile. "Who is that?"

He nodded diplomatically as he pulled her into the room crowded with friends and business associates. Political connections, allies, the powerful and the rich from all corners of Britain, mortal and immortal alike. "That, luv, is my good friend, Father Banner."

"That is a priest, Terrance. A *priest*." Her cheeks were sore from smiling.

"Well, of course it is, luv." They reached the front of the room and Terry locked his intense blue eyes with hers. "I want to do this properly."

Sad, really. She liked London. But Gemma was going to have to kill him.

CHAPTER THREE

"I will never share your day-chamber again."

"Is that a promise?" He cocked an eyebrow at her. She hated going back on her word, so if she was actually promising... Terry might have been screwed. Or not, as the case may be. "It was meant to be a pleasant surprise, luv."

She clamped her mouth shut, but her blue eyes turned frosty in the balmy air. Though Gemma didn't know where they were, they were actually headed to her favorite vacation house on the coast of Northern Spain. The air and water were growing warmer. Sadly, she'd decided to put on clothes.

She looked around. "I could always swim to shore."

"Think you could get there by sunrise?"

She glared. "Maybe."

"I'd hate to be wrong on that one. Know where we are?" He glanced up. "It is a clear night. How're your navigation skills?"

His were excellent. He'd resisted learning to sail for years, preferring the fresh waters he'd been born near, but once he'd finally given in, Terry discovered a passion for the sea. This particular boat was his favorite. It was docked in a very private location. No one except Carl and Roger even knew he owned it. *The Conquest* was a 35 foot sailing vessel he could manage himself. Truthfully, he could steer any boat smaller than a freighter with his elemental ability, but it just took a bit longer than this swift little prize. Gemma had never stepped foot on it.

"How did you get me into that chamber?"

"With help."

"Are we secure here?"

Ever the security conscious vampire, he'd known she would raise the question. The fact that she was just as fierce about his security was the part that gave him hope. "We are on a ship that only two beings know about. You didn't even know about it prior to this evening, so that should tell you something. There is a single secured day chamber that can only be accessed by a trap door in the bottom of the hull."

"I noticed."

"So you did. We have enough supplies here for three months of independent living, should we choose it."

Her breath caught. "You're not going to keep me here for three months, are you?"

Of course not. "Maybe."

"You can't be serious! Who's running things at home?"

"Roger and Mina, of course. Max and Cathy are staying for security, should anything come up."

Gemma nodded. "That was a good choice. It's a good-will gesture from us toward the MacGregors, and no one will cause problems with Cathy around. Roger can take care of the day-to-day. Mina has all the details for... yes, this might not be an utter disaster."

"Never seen a woman so opposed to a vacation. You work too much, Gem."

"And Max will take care of Daniel. Make sure he

doesn't cause any problems. He could smooth things over with anyone who's angry..."

He finally saw her start to relax. She trusted her family more than she did him. It irked him, even though he knew it shouldn't.

After all, one of the reasons Terry had pursued Gemma was because of her family, and not for the reasons she suspected. Yes, Carwyn's clan was hugely influential and powerful, but they also reminded Terry of his own human family. It was that dependability and trust he'd hungered for in their connection at first. Now, of course, it was much more.

But he wished she trusted him more. In hindsight, that might be one drawback to the whole kidnapping scheme. Still, one did what was necessary to achieve the desired results. Gemma was here, on his favorite boat, and he was going to spend the next week seducing her into falling in love with him.

Not a bad plan, really. He just hoped it worked.

Gemma was staring over the water. "Who had access to me while I was in day rest, Terry?"

His head fell back in frustration. "No one I don't trust implicitly."

"Who?"

He snapped down the book he'd been reading. "Why? So you can kill them?"

"Maybe."

He shook his head and picked up the biography again. "No."

"I knew I should have never stayed with you yesterday. Serves me right for being sentimental. I won't make that mistake again."

It set his teeth on edge, but he swallowed his anger. "There's only one secure day-chamber on this vessel, so you'll have to share unless you want to spend the day at the bottom of the ocean, Gemma."

She sipped the blood-wine he'd stored in the galley. "I still can't believe you kidnapped me."

Time to change the subject. "How's that batch?"

She gave a noncommittal shrug and rose to pace the deck. "Better, but I still think Rene could do more with the flavor of the port. The blood... actually tastes quite good. Very little of the normal staleness."

Blood wine was their newest venture, and one that Terry hoped to have ready for export within the year. Vampires had experimented with preserving blood in alcohol for hundreds of years with mixed results, most of them bad. Wine, possibly for color reasons, was the most popular, but tended to leave the blood stale. Gemma had hired a brandy distiller from France two years before with the idea that a distilled liquor would have better results. Brandy hadn't worked as well as she'd hoped, but port seemed to have real possibilities. The fortified wine's sweet flavor masked the staleness of the blood and the higher alcohol content had kept some batches preserved for almost six months in a traditional wine cellar. If they produced it successfully, they would become some of the richest vampires in the world.

"Give me a taste?" He reached out a hand, aching to have her closer, even if she was just sharing a drink.

She wandered over, the white shift she'd put on fluttering in the night wind. He swallowed hard. She held the glass out, and Terry snatched it from her fingers before he pulled her down to his lap. She sat with a huff, but he nudged her chin up, pressing a soft kiss to the spot on her neck he knew she loved. Then he lifted the glass to her lips.

"Drink."

She did. He pulled the glass away before he ran his tongue along the seam of her lips, tasting the heady sweetness before he captured her mouth. He pulled back, taking a drink himself so his mouth was stained with the rich taste of the blood and wine. Gemma followed the scent, and he saw her fangs descend. She hungered. For him. For blood. He'd give her a taste, but it wasn't time to slake her thirst just yet.

"Gemma?" His hand ran to the nape of her neck, tugging on the damp hair until he'd taken her lips again.

"Yes?"

"I want..."

Her heart was thumping steadily and it made him grin. "What?" she panted.

Terry pulled back and took a deep breath. "Dinner. You hungry?"

She blinked. "I... what?"

He set her on her feet and gave her bum an affectionate pat. "I'll just make something light. You relax, luv. Enjoy the wine. That batch really is better. Might have to give the Frenchman a raise." Then Terry left her stunned and slipped into the galley to poach the fish he'd caught earlier. This was going better than he'd expected.

"Bon appetit."

He set the dish down in front of her. It was a light meal consisting of bluefish poached in white wine with some fruit on the side. As a younger vampire, Terry still enjoyed food more than Gemma did, but she did need a bit in her stomach to remain comfortable. Occasionally, he tried to imagine her as human, but he just couldn't. She was the embodiment of immortal beauty to him. Everything about her screamed ferocious blood-sucking predator. No wonder he was in love.

"Is it all right, Gem?"

She frowned a little, looking at the table. "It's fine. Thank you, Terry."

Why'd she gone all quiet and soft? That wasn't like her at all. "Gobsmacked again, eh? Sorry. I know you don't like being surprised by my many talents. I'll try to be more considerate in the future."

And just like that, her eyes sparked. "I was trying to think of a gentle way to tell you that your French accent sounds like a nineteenth century whore, but there just isn't one, is there?"

Terry grinned. There she was. "That might tell you where I learned it, luv."

"I'd say, 'Do tell.' But I'd really rather you didn't."

"I speak it. That's all that's important. *Você não acha?*"

He'd forced a smile out of her. "Your Portuguese is rather nice, though."

"That's because I like the language more."

She shook her head and little and tasted the fish. "It's not always about indulging your own wishes, Terry. France is an important trading partner and if we're going to continue to cultivate Jean Desmarais as an ally—"

"It's all about indulging myself *on my honeymoon.* How's the fish? Caught it earlier. Thought it might go well with those figs and the new wine."

"Excellent." She set her fork down and just looked at him.

"What?"

"You never cook at home."

"We employ a cook at home. And I'm very busy." He squirmed a little under her unwavering gaze. "So?"

"You're a very good cook."

"I have to be. Someday, I might not be able to afford domestic help, and I have a very demanding wife."

"That's so likely, *husband*."

Mercy, he wanted to take her on the table right then. He loved calling her his wife. Loved it almost as much as the little curl her lip made when she heard the word. He was such a contrary ass sometimes.

She was still examining him. "We do have an excellent cook at home."

"We do."

"Whom you hired yourself."

He narrowed his eyes. What was she getting at? "Yes..."

She grabbed him and pulled him over the table, licking up the side of his neck as Terry shivered. Then Gemma whispered in his ear, "You, Terrance Ramsay, are..."

Fuck, he knew she could hear his heart pounding. "I'm what?"

She bit his earlobe. "A snob."

Gemma pushed him away before he could grab her. "I am not!"

She laughed. What had gotten into her? Whatever it was, he liked it. He tried to quash the smile that threatened his lips.

"You are," she said. "You're a *food* snob, aren't you?"

"Not a snob. I just like good food."

"Oh really? Because I saw the face you made at that dinner with the German club owners—" Terry couldn't stop the wince. The beef had been dry to the point of jerky. And they should never have served that wine with dinner.

"Ha!" Gemma crowed. "I thought it was the company, but it wasn't. It was the food!"

"It was the company, too."

She took another bite of the fish. "You're a food snob. How very aristocratic of you, Terrance."

"It's not snobbish to dislike over-spiced roast which tasted as if it had been run over with—" Gemma burst into laughter. "What do you know? You hardly eat anything."

"I think it's rather adorable. Do you have an apron? Watch the cooking programs while I'm out of the house?"

Forget the food. He threw his napkin down and stood, but she beat him to her feet and darted into the cabin. So they were playing that game? Terry's blood sang. He loved a chase, and in the enclosed space, neither one of them could hide for long.

I love you. I want you. Be mine. I want you to be mine.

"Gemma," he called tauntingly. "I can smell you, luv."

She darted by, scratching one nail along his neck and whispering, "I can smell you, too." Then she sped outside.

His fangs lowered at the quick bite of pain. He wanted her to latch onto it and suck. He wanted the bite of her fangs in his skin as she drank and licked and... The growl ripped from his throat when he caught her scent on the breeze and his eyes turned toward the bow. There. A white finger curled over the rail. She was hanging over the port side. He stripped off the loose pants he'd been wearing and slipped silently into the water, moving around the boat until he was right under her, then Terry leapt up and grabbed her legs, pulling her into the sea.

She fought him, twisting in the black water until the bubbles churned around them both, fighting up toward the surface, but he pulled her back down with a laugh. Her heart was thumping, and her amnis...

Suddenly Terry stilled. She continued to fight him, slashing her nails toward his throat and trying to fight out of his grip.

She was frightened.

He spun her around in his arms and shouted, "*Gemma!*" as loud as he could under the water. His amnis reached out and enfolded her body, which was stiff as a board. She clutched at his neck with wide eyes.

"You're fine," he said again, the last of the air leaving his lungs as he continued to try to sooth her. *I have you,* he mouthed. *I have you.*

Why was she frightened? She could stay underwater for hours, if she wanted. Hadn't she ever tried it? Surely, at some point...

Gemma was frozen in his arms, wrapped in his power and slowly coming out of the unexpected panic. He swam toward the small trap door on the hull, pressing the hidden buttons that would release the catch,

41

then he pulled her in and held her against him as he waited for the hatch to close behind him and the water to drain. When it did, he released the second set of doors, dragging a silent Gemma into the cozy paneled chamber that took the place of the stateroom.

"Gemma?" He grabbed a towel and stripped her clothes off. He was cold, dammit. His skin usually matched the temperature of the air around him, which meant at the moment it was as cool as the water they'd been swimming in. It would take a while for his amnis to warm his body up. "Gemma?"

"I'm fine." She snatched the towel from his hands and twisted away. "You just surprised me."

"Why are you scared of water?"

He should have been expecting the punch, but it knocked him back into the luxurious pillows in the corner of the room.

"I'm not afraid of water. It can't hurt me."

"I know that."

She sniffed and pressed the towel to her face. "You surprised me. That's all. Well done."

Not well done at all, in his opinion, but he didn't press the point. If Gemma didn't want to admit the weakness to him, it was her business.

Or was it? He was her husband. Her partner. Still, he was reluctant to shatter whatever had bloomed between them at dinner. For a few minutes, they'd been relaxed. Playful. Neither trying to best the other. It hadn't been a battle of wits or bodies, but a delicate kind of dance they were both enjoying.

Then he had to fuck it up.

She'd never been strictly comfortable around water.

She was an earth vampire, obviously, so it wasn't her element, but it couldn't kill her. Had she drowned in her human life? When Gemma was human, swimming wasn't something women usually learned. He knew she was from inland. Terry had grown up along a river and had been at home in the water for as long as he could remember.

"I'm sorry," he finally said. "If you like, I'll find shelter somewhere else. The bedroom is yours."

Her shoulders relaxed a little. "It's fine."

"No, it's not."

"You don't have to sleep in the water, Terry."

He tried to lighten the mood. "Do I get points for offering?"

A glint came back to her eyes. "No."

"Why not?" He rose and walked to her, flicking on the small heater to banish the chill from the damp air. He grabbed another towel from a cupboard and knelt down, looking up as he ran the soft cotton over her legs.

"Because..." Her eyes softened as she watched him.

Over her knees. Up her thighs. The towel draped over his hands as he slowly stood, running his fingers over her damp skin. Her hips and belly.

"Because why?"

He didn't even remember what they'd been talking about. Lord, he wanted her. He was hard as a rock and aching to be in her, but Terry held himself back. He was more interested in banishing the tension from her shoulders, the guarded expression from her eyes. He slowly moved the towel up her body until he was standing in front of her.

"Because..."

"Will you stay with me today, Gemma?"

"Promise not to kidnap me again?"

He smiled and pressed the length of her hair between his hands to dry it. "Promise." He draped the towel over her shoulders and rubbed his hands over her arms.

"Then I'll stay. For now."

Stay forever. He bent down and kissed her, his desire tightly leashed as he tortured her with soft lips and gentle hands. He felt her try to pull them back into more aggressive territory as she walked him to the bed, but Terry would not be deterred. He continued to meet her demanding lips with gentleness. It was too easy, he realized. Too easy to grab for the flash and the explosion when he wanted the low, slow burn of desire between them. Terry wanted more.

He wanted more of Gemma, not the body she offered, but the heart she guarded.

Terry wanted it, and he would have it.

Or, she might kill him when she found out he had no intention of ever letting her leave him. That was a definite possibility, too.

CHAPTER FOUR

London, 1885

Gemma was late for the party. She hated being late. Ironically, that night she was purposefully late. It wouldn't do to arrive at Juliette's early. After all, she hadn't been seen in London immortal society for over fifteen years. An entrance was called for.

As the coach rolled up to the glittering house outside of the city, Gemma wondered again at the multiple invitations to the high society party. Francis Winthrop had asked her to accompany him. She'd debated for a few moments, but considering she didn't want her first appearance back in London to be in the retinue of the current vampire lord, Gemma declined. Their hostess for the evening, an old friend, had already invited her. She would see Francis there. Maybe she'd be able to ascertain why, exactly, he wanted Gemma at his side.

The door to the carriage opened. "Ms. Melcombe. Welcome."

"Thank you." She accepted the gracious hand down, thankful for the more understated bustle she'd brought from Paris. The English fashions were ridiculously unwieldy.

"If you would come this way, Ms. Melcombe." The human held out a hand toward the glittering entrance.

He smelled absolutely mouth-watering.

Julie, Julie, what are you feeding the help these days? A small smile flirted around her mouth. *And can I borrow this one for the evening?*

She saw the hostess almost immediately upon entering the house. "Mrs. Daubry!" She walked toward Juliette. "How are you?"

Her old friend held out a hand, then greeted her with a kiss on both cheeks, much to Gemma's pleasure. "You smell like Paris. I'm horribly jealous." Her friend's accent may have faded in her seventy years in England, but every now and then, Juliette Daubry let it out to play.

"It's the perfume, my dear. I have a wonderful new man that makes it for me. Very keen nose for a human."

Juliette sent a careless wave toward her husband, a minor earl that someone had turned around forty years before, probably for his fortune. Luckily, the Englishman had enough sense to remain alive long enough to marry her friend, who was older and more savvy about vampire politics. They seemed happy enough, in Gemma's opinion. A good match for them both, though one that Gemma did not envy in the least.

The two vampires linked arms and began to stroll the room.

"We haven't had a chance to meet until now," Gemma said in a low voice, conscious of the many ears around them. "What have I missed?"

"Very little. You know how it is." Juliette waved an arm around the room. "Look at all these beautiful old people. Lovely, rich, and boring. Tell me about Paris. Things are always more interesting there."

"And more unstable. Why did Francis ask me to

accompany him tonight? Is his position secure? Is my information faulty?" Gemma had long been accustomed to vampires in power, particularly males, courting her favor. Her sire was one of the oldest in the British Isles. Her brother was the power behind anyone who ruled Ireland. She had two brothers in Northern France who were quickly making names for themselves. Gemma's clan was powerful and rich. Attention was to be expected, but she'd moved back to London to enjoy a break from politics.

"Francis is fine," Juliette said. "I'm trying to think of any major challenge in the last ten years, to be honest. There hasn't been, that I know of. Probably in part due to his new second."

"Who is it?"

"A nobody." Juliette shrugged at Gemma's questioning look. "Truly. No one knows where he comes from. He's certainly English, according to his horrid accent, but other than that..." Another lazy shrug and a pout. "No one knows."

"Water vampire?"

"Of course. Everyone assumes Francis sired him after he found him in a dingy alley, but no one asks."

"Naturally." Gemma's eyes scanned the room for new faces. There were a sprinkling of unfamiliars, but all in the company of vampires Gemma knew. Lots of humans, some for sport and others present for their business of social connections. No one who fit Juliette's description.

"Is he loyal?" For some reason, the hair on the back of her neck stood on end. Someone was watching her. She whipped her head around, but spotted no one.

Juliette's attention had been drawn across the room by a pair of humans in military attire. "Who?"

Gemma smiled to herself. Her friend always did have a taste for a man in uniform. "This new second, is he loyal to Francis?"

She may not have wanted the close connection that Francis did, but she did like the vampire. She considered him a friend. Even more, he was a known entity. Gemma had just moved back to England. She didn't relish having to navigate through an unfamiliar power structure when she'd rather be exploring the new shops or riding the horse she'd just had transported from Belgium.

"Follows him around like a loyal guard dog." Juliette narrowed in on the two humans. "I don't think you have anything to worry about. I'm famished, my friend. You?"

Gemma eyed the two men. One was tall and blond, the other had dark curls that reminded her of someone she knew. "How very indelicate to mention it, Julie. The dark one is mine."

"Greedy." The men stood, red-faced by the women's obvious attentions.

"Come, Major." Juliette once again took advantage of her fetching accent and laid a bare hand on the man's wrist. "Come with me."

Blinking through the amnis that had flooded his mind, the blond officer nodded. Gemma quickly laid her hands on the other, leading him to the garden where a dark corner waited. She felt her fangs grow long as the man's scent hit her nose. She'd been waiting for days to truly drink, knowing that Juliette always had the most delicious humans at her parties. But as she sunk her fangs into the man's soft neck and he let out a quiet groan of pleasure, she felt it again.

Watching. Someone was watching her. There was a frisson of energy that snaked toward her, even as she drank her fill of the rich blood in her arms. A teasing, testing waft of amnis curled and twisted along the ground. It snaked along her angles in the misty night, until Gemma spun, furious to be distracted from her meal. She heard the human sag against the hedge.

"Who disturbs me?" she said just loud enough to be heard.

She heard his low laugh as he walked out of the fog. "So sorry to interrupt your meal, m'lady."

The vampire was nothing more than a looming shadow outlined by the lights of the house. He stood like a dark omen with the evening fog swirling around him. Gemma lifted her chin, making no move to wipe away the blood she could feel at the edge of her mouth. Her fangs were still long and throbbing.

"I highly doubt you are truly sorry. And I am no lady."

"Is that so?" He stepped forward and Gemma forced herself to remain still. "That's the best news I've heard tonight."

Her lip curled for a moment, but when the unknown vampire walked out of the shadows, she closed her mouth to conceal her reaction.

Power.

He radiated it. It was young and untamed, but it poured off him in waves. Not the old, formidable strength she'd come to associate with the oldest of their kind, but a quick lash that seemed to spark and jump around him. A water vampire. The evening fog clung to him, curling around his legs like a cat as he strode through the night.

His eyes locked with hers. Young, yes, but not intimidated. His eyes were blue-grey like the northern oceans, and his body was powerful. Broad shoulders over narrow hips. Strong legs. An athlete's body. Unlike most men in her circles, this man made no effort to conceal his brute strength. Gemma doubted he could have if he tried. His sandy hair was not combed fashionably, but cropped close to his head, and his cheeks sported a dark stubble that told Gemma he had little use for the careful grooming most vampires adhered to in the modern age.

"Who are you?"

"My employer would very much like a moment of your time, Ms. Melcombe."

"That's lovely," she sneered. "But you have me at a disadvantage, sir. We have not been introduced."

"I very much doubt any man catches you at a true disadvantage." He nodded to the woozy officer with a slight smile. "Doesn't look like you have many complaints, though."

He may have had a wealth of raw, young power, but it was nothing compared to her strength. She bared her fangs. "Your name."

The vampire stepped forward, his eyes sparking at her show of aggression. She could see his fangs grow long behind his lips.

He held out a hand. "Terrance Ramsay, Ms. Melcombe. Faithful second of Lord Francis Winthrop, vampire lord of London."

So this was Francis's new guard dog. How amusing. He did appear loyal... if a little untamed. She held out her own hand, no need to be impolite, despite the indelicacy of their initial meeting. She wouldn't want to offend the current leader of the city. "Mr. Ramsay, I—"

She broke off as soon as he took her fingers with his own. The sharp spike of energy caused the dark garden to spin, just for a second. He bent over her hand, touching his lips to the back of her knuckles, lingering longer than was strictly polite. Then Terrance Ramsay looked up, meeting her eyes with a predator's hungry stare.

What was this? He looked as shocked as she did. Her heart gave a completely involuntary thud and a shocking warmth spread through her belly.

"Let go of my hand," she said softly.

His fingers squeezed tighter for a moment, then he blinked and released her. "Of course."

"Francis wants to see me, I take it?"

He stiffened at the use of his employer's Christian name. "You two are friends? Have you known each other long?"

"You'll find that it's best not to ask questions like that." Gemma left the officer in the bushes. Let Juliette's staff clean up the mess. "But yes, Francis and I were friends when you were a human babe nursing at your mother's breast, Mr. Ramsay."

He only looked amused. "Then you're looking well, Ms. Melcombe. For your age."

Gemma smirked. "Human women are offended by references to their age. I, however, am not human."

The younger vampire turned to her as he held open the door. His fangs were still long, and he let them peek from behind his lips. "Clearly not. How fortunate."

Did Francis's new vampire think to pursue her? How... amusing. And naive. Did he think an immortal of her age and power needed to be saddled with a young thing like him? Did he think she needed protecting? The thought made her laugh out loud.

"You're young, Mr. Ramsay. You'll learn that appearances can be very deceiving."

"Care to teach me?" His eyes lingered at the bare skin of her throat. "I imagine you'd find me a very... thorough pupil."

Gemma's nostrils flared slightly at the smell of arousal that had unexpectedly filled the air. Impertinent, arrogant, cocky—

"Gemma, darling!" Francis appeared at her side, leaning down and kissing her cheek as Gemma tore her eyes from the unexpected challenge in his gaze. "It is so good to see you. And you've met Terry, I see."

"Wonderful to see you, as well." She turned her back on the young water vampire and walked with her old friend. "I'm looking forward to being back in London, Francis."

"And I'm looking forward to having you here, darling. It's been too long." They strolled back into the crowd, chatting with friends and associates as Gemma reacquainted herself with London society. She spun and danced. Flirted and joked. It was, all in all, a very pleasant homecoming.

And Gemma felt Terrance Ramsay's eyes on her all night long.

Present day

"I'm remarkably bored." She stared out over the water. The moon was full and reflecting on the soft waves as the boat sped through the water heading... she had no idea where. "I can't remember the last time I was bored."

"That's because you work. All the time." He was doing some ridiculous thing with sails and rope and rigging. She hated boats. Hated everything about the ocean. The few times she had to board them, she found a secluded room and read a book or played cards. Usually, if she had to travel, she dragged work along with her. Or Terry. He could be remarkably entertaining if he wanted to be. At the moment, he seemed to want to lecture her more.

"—why we do all this, Gem. Honestly, if you can't enjoy yourself sometimes, than what's the point of this life?"

"Survival. Acquisition. The safety of my family and those under my aegis."

He had no ready answer for that, but he pursed his lips in displeasure. "You need to relax, luv."

"Does relaxing equal boredom?" She stretched out on the cushioned bench that ran around the bow. "Because if that's the case, I'm *very* relaxed."

"Want to learn how to sail the boat?"

"Not particularly."

He laughed. "Then sit back and—"

"Relax. Yes, you've mentioned that. Do we, in fact, have a destination in mind?"

"We do."

"And will there be things to do there?"

His smile turned to a wicked grin. "Other than me?"

And there it was. The sharp spike of desire flared just as it had every night they'd been on the ocean. And just as predictably, he left it there hanging. Terry was being... unusually standoffish. Distant, in a way. She hated it. All he had to was touch her and she was wild with desire for him, but he... It almost seemed as if he didn't want her at times. He'd always been in control of their sexual relationship, which annoyed her to no end. They were equals in every way but that.

Suddenly angry, she turned away from him and stared out at the ocean again.

"Oy!" he barked. "What was that?"

"Nothing." She made her voice as toneless as possible.

"Not nothing. Do you think I'm an idiot?"

"Sometimes," she muttered under her breath. Then more loudly, "I'm fine. I told you, I'm bored."

But maybe she could think of a way to distract him. Then she wouldn't be bored. Gemma slowly began to unbutton the sheer white blouse she'd put on that night. She heard Terry shift behind her.

He gave a low hum. "Hmm."

"Enjoying the view?" She slipped the shirt off her shoulders so she was in nothing but a small string bikini and a loose skirt.

"From the moment I met you."

She glanced over her shoulder. "Hard to appreciate much with those old dresses."

"I have a good imagination."

Gemma couldn't hold back the laugh. "True."

"I'm using it right now, as a matter of fact."

"Is that so." She slipped off the skirt. "Is that

helping?"

"It's certainly helping one thing along, luv."

Rolling over, she stared at him, flicking her eyes up and down his body possessively. *Hers.* The thought was surprisingly satisfying. And annoying. Terry was her partner, it wouldn't do to let her more base instincts take control. Emotions like that only led to broken hearts and tragedy.

"Come here," she murmured. "I want you."

A smile flirted at the corner of his mouth. "I'm yours."

Her breath caught; her heart gave an excited thump. Still, she swallowed her emotion and slid the straps of her bathing suit off her shoulders. "Show me."

Terry's eyes left the ocean and met hers. Hungry. Predatory. It was the stare she loved. The stare that told her, no matter how he acted at times, he wanted her just as much as she wanted him. He did something with the wheel, then sauntered over the deck, turning up the music as he walked. A sultry Spanish voice filled the air.

She slipped the rest of her suit off and said, "Your turn." He was wearing a loose button down shirt and a pair of linen pants. She could see him stiff and aching for her. "Take them off."

"No." He pulled her up and into his chest, wrapping one arm tight around her waist as the other grabbed her hand.

Gemma blinked. "What are you doing?"

"Dancing," he said. "With my wife."

"This isn't the kind of dancing I had in mind."

He swayed to the music, leading her as his thumb trailed down her spine. "We'll get there."

Why was he being like this? It set her fangs on edge, even as his hands seduced her body. Their legs brushed together and she felt the length of him pressed against her belly. The feel of him fully clothed against her bare skin was almost unbearably erotic. Every nerve in her body was on edge.

"Terry—"

"Shhhh," he whispered as he bent down and kissed her. Slow, slow, slow. "No rush, luv."

Rush! She wanted to scream. *Release me from this maddening need, you ass!*

She tried to reach for the button on his pants, but he caught her hands, holding them captive as he made love to her mouth. Gemma's heart almost crashed out of her chest at the sudden realization. That's what he was doing.

He was making love to her.

The bastard.

She tried to pull her mouth away, but... his tongue was curled against hers, first stroking sensuously, then flicking the edge of her lengthened fang. His hand had softened around her wrists and his thumb stroked the tender skin. His other hand slid down, caressing over the curve of her bottom until he'd reached her thigh, which he hitched up, spreading her legs so his hips rested between hers. Still, he made no move to undress and the throbbing at her center turned to an ache.

The music had switched to a slow tango that tugged at her memories. Terry held her leg up and pressed his hand to the small of her back, holding her there for one, agonizing moment. Then he let her leg down and spun her around, so her bare back was pressed into his chest and his arms wrapped around her waist.

"Do you remember?" he whispered in her ear. "That club in Santiago?"

"Yes."

"You thought I wouldn't learn to tango." He began to sway with the music, running his hands down her bare arms as his stubbled chin scraped the nape of her neck.

"You told me once you weren't a dancer."

Grabbing her hand, he spun her around and forced her eyes to his as the music sped up. "Only with you."

He grabbed her around the waist, kicking her leg out and nudging her into the steps they'd learned together. The deck was small, so he kept the movements close, pausing every now and then to kiss her breathless. And he still made no move to take his clothes off.

"What do you think you're doing?" she asked when the song ended. He held her, watching as Gemma finally lost patience and ripped the shirt from his body. "Why are you being like this?"

He slid his belt out and she pulled at the waistband until his pants slipped down his legs and he stepped out of them, taking her down to the deck in one smooth movement. "I'm changing the rules, Gemma."

She froze for a second until his mouth latched on to her neck and her body arched in need. "What?"

Gemma could barely hear his low, rough voice when he said, "I want more."

How did she knew he didn't mean sex? She gulped. "You knew what I was offering when I agreed to this."

"I know." His fangs scraped along the sensitive skin between her breasts, not breaking the skin, but causing her to shiver. Her blood welled just beneath the surface, aching for his mouth. His fingers reached down, testing and teasing before he slid into her with a slow thrust that almost brought tears to her eyes. "I've decided I want more. And I'm going to get it."

How could he do this to her? Gemma wanted to scream from pleasure and fury, all at the same time. She hated him. She wanted him. She loved—no, she didn't love Terry. She couldn't. Still, even as she raged on the inside, he controlled her body, moving slowly, wrapping her legs around him as he played her with perfect control.

"Not fair," she cried. "You're not playing—"

"Fuck fair," he growled, suddenly speeding up. "This isn't a game."

Close, she was so close. "Terry, don't—"

"I lied, stole, and killed to win the power I wield now, Gemma." She wrapped her hands around his wrists and came with violent shudder, but Terry didn't stop. He only bent down to whisper in her ear, "What makes you think I would do any less to win you?"

"I can't—"

Though her mind was screaming, he stopped her mouth with a furious kiss, holding Gemma to his chest as her mind and heart raced around what he was saying. Then Terry's lips softened; he shifted over her and smiled. "Again."

CHAPTER FIVE

London, 1923

He could hear the drip, drip, drip of the blood as it fell into the canal leading from the river to his sire's underground residence beneath the Temple. Terry ignored the fetid smell of the Thames and tossed the body into the pile ringed by wide-eyed vampires from London's elite. He spit the last of the traitor's blood to the ground, flicking his knife as he walked around the gaping immortal populace.

"Bring in the next one."

Denton and Max muscled in another of his late brother's conspirators. This one he recognized.

"Burke. Nice of you to come by the old place." The chambers north of the Thames didn't see much activity. No, his sire had maintained more luxurious houses in fashionable parts of town. He'd thrown lavish parties that the aristocracy had attended. Francis Winthrop had been a gentleman—a powerful vampire—but one who saw the more civilized of their kind as his peers. That had been what killed him.

The pain screamed from his chest. His sire was dead, killed by a traitor with the face of a friend. Even Terry had been taken in by his deception. And to discover that his own brother—Winthrop's only other child—had been behind it...

Terry gripped the shivering earth vampire by the hair. "Do you have anything to say to this lot?"

"You're a monster."

"Aye, that I am." He pulled the vampire close, whispering in his ear as he slowly slit Burke's throat. "And none of them will forget it."

The assassin was dead, killed within minutes of Winthrop's death. But it hadn't brought his sire back. Terry, along with his first, Roger, had ordered Winthrop's men to scour the black streets of London, their fury matched only by their loyalty to their fallen leader. The vampires who hadn't been able to flee were snatched from the streets, even taken by Terry's human staff during the daytime, then woken in the old basement fortress to watch as Terry systematically killed every suspect in his sire's death. Slowly. He extracted each bit of information for the benefit of his glittering, sophisticated audience. Even the oldest of them appeared horrified at his brutality.

Which was exactly as Terry had wanted it.

By the third night, none of them appeared squeamish anymore. None of them met his eye in challenge. None of them batted an eye when he called himself their lord.

The blood poured down the chest of the traitor, dripping onto Terry's shoes. The ground was thick with blood, earth, and ash, turned to a fetid mud by the water drawn into the room with Terry's cold fury. With a quick snap, his knife dug into the back of the vampire's neck, severing the spine as Terry watched the amnis flicker out. A fleck of blood hit his cheek as his victim heaved a last rattling breath through his severed windpipe.

Terry tossed the body onto the pile. The first of his public executions, including his own brother, were disintegrating at the base of the pile, returning to whatever element had sustained them. A slow seep of water was the last trace of the man who had once been his closest friend.

"Next."

Before another traitor could be brought before him, Roger slipped over and whispered in his ear. "Boss, you have a visitor."

"Not the best time, Roger."

"Pardon me presuming, but I think you'll want to see this one."

Their eyes met for a moment before Terry nodded. If Roger had interrupted him, it had to be important.

He strode from the room, grabbing his grey jacket which hung on the arm of another of his brutes. "Keep them here. If they get hungry, let them feed on the prisoners."

"Yes, Boss."

Terry walked up the stairs, into the grey law offices that had hidden the oldest of his sire's hideaways. The Temple building had been Winthrop's place for the nasty business. The place he hadn't utilized near enough in the years Terry had been with him. If he had, maybe he wouldn't be...

He took a moment to lean against the wall, momentarily overwhelmed by his grief. The tears leaked from the corners of his eyes unashamedly. He'd loved Francis Winthrop as a father. The man had taken him in as a human, trained him, educated him, trying to mold the rough human into a loyal guard. He'd seen potential in a way that no other had. Then, he'd turned him into the powerful creature Terry had become. And now his sire was no more.

He heard a soft shuffle of feet at the door. She was letting him know she was there. As if her amnis hadn't already announced her. As if the reaction of his body hadn't already given her away. The office door opened and he lifted bloody eyes to Gemma Melcombe. They stood for a moment, staring at each other. What was there to say?

"I am so terribly sorry about Francis." She looked it, too. Good acting? Or something sincere? It wasn't often the Ice Queen let her emotions out of the tight little box she'd perfected. He envied her that. Terry waved away the guard so they had some privacy.

"Where have you been?"

"Out of town, helping my father with a new member of our clan."

"For a year?"

She stepped forward, and Terry caught a glimpse of her slight figure underneath the pale blue dress. The current fashions suited her refined beauty. Everything suited her. Always had. "Feel free to verify that, if you must, but I had nothing to do with Francis's death. And even if I'd been here, I never suspected—"

"Aye, none of us did." He rubbed a hand over his jaw and moved to the desk at the center of the room, trying to ignore his reaction to her. Over fifty years acquaintance had proven it was not something she shared. Still, unlike the others he dealt with lately, Gemma had been a true, if wary, friend of Winthrop's.

"Why are you here, Ms. Melcombe?"

"You have a boy in custody."

"I have many in custody. They're mine by conquest."

"No one is disputing that. I came here to ask for mercy."

The Ice Queen wanted a favor of him? His grieving heart wanted to reject it. His brain told him to hear her out.

"Who is it?"

"A kinsman's youngest son. A member of my clan. He is... young. And not the most circumspect in his connections."

"You could say that. The name?"

"Rene. Rene Dupont. He is my brother Guy's youngest child."

"How do you know I haven't killed him already?"

She paused. "Have you?"

Terry held her blue eyes for a few long moments. "No."

"Then I ask for mercy."

"Why should I give him mercy? I've killed everyone even remotely connected with my sire's death. Why should he be different?"

"He is only twenty years immortal. He fell in with foolish friends, but he has no ambition. I promise, he was not a part of the plot to murder your sire. He was drawn in by his crowd. That is all."

Terry leaned back and closed his eyes. If he could feel exhausted, he would. As it was, it was summer and the nights were short. He had little time to deal with the problems in front of him before his human security would have to take over.

"Ms. Melcombe—"

"Terry." She stepped forward, her eyes pleading. "Francis was my friend. I would never intervene if I thought the boy had anything to do with his death. Guy is frantic. He will make restitution for his son's actions. His business in France is not insubstantial, nor is his influence. He can offer money—"

"I don't want your bloody money." His voice was low and furious. "Is that why you're here? To offer me money?"

Her jaw tightened and her eyes narrowed. "What do you want?"

"From your brother? Nothing." He didn't need allies in France, but for the clan of Carwyn ap Bryn to owe the new leader of London a favor...

He could almost see Gemma's mind working behind her clear gaze. "Who then? My father? You want his support? You're the new leader of London. You're young." Her face came alive at the political manipulations. "If you agree to release Rene, my father could throw his support behind you. My brother in Ireland—"

"You've powerful family in Scotland, as well." Terry should have known she'd figure it out quickly. *So smart.* His blood stirred at the sight of her.

"I do." Her eyes lit in triumph. "So, do we have a deal? Rene's freedom for the tacit approval of your succession?"

Such a clever girl. Was it wrong that he wanted to ruffle her just to get a reaction?

"No."

She blinked in surprise. "No?"

"No." He felt a tickling on his cheek. It was the blood of his most recent victim starting to dry. He wiped it away with the back of his fingers, knowing a smear of red would remain. Good. Let her see it. "I have the city. I don't need your clan's approval."

"We're not offering approval, Mr. Ramsay—"

"Good. I was Winthrop's son and second for over sixty years. I avenged his death. I have killed the majority of my enemies in front of the city's population. I do not need your approval to take over."

Her lip began to curl in disdain. "So you mean to reject the support of my family and—"

"Your family would have supported me anyway, Ms. Melcombe. *They* have nothing I want or need."

She didn't miss his emphasis. He tried not to smile. In the chaos and grief of the past three nights, sparring with Gemma Melcombe was a bright spot of light.

"*They* don't have anything you need?"

"Nothing that would tempt me to release Rene." Let her think he'd been planning to kill the boy. He hadn't decided one way or another until she'd showed up. Knowing the young vampire's age and connections would have been enough to sway him, but then she'd started offering all sorts of bribes he hadn't even planned on. He was curious what she'd offer next.

She took a cautious step forward, her eyes growing colder by the minute. "And what would tempt you?"

He smirked. "Lots of things, luv."

"Is that so?"

She was so damn proper. But that fire behind her eyes... it drew him in. She may have been cold and impersonal on the outside, but Terry would bet she was a thing of beauty when riled. How much, exactly, would it take to rile her?

"Have anything on you, Gemma?" Bloody hell, her name tasted sweet in his mouth. He wanted to say it again. Wanted to shout it. Moan it. Tease his own name from her lips. "Anything that might tempt me?"

Faster than he could blink, she leaned forward, baring her fangs. "You foolish boy! I come here offering a fair bargain, and you throw it in my face? Who do you think you are?"

He stood, deliberately calm though the blood rushed in his veins. "I'm the vampire who holds your brother's child. I'm the lord of this city now, and I'm the man who has a dozen vicious guards, human and vampire, within shouting distance."

"That only works if you have a tongue to shout, impudent boy."

Terry couldn't hold back the shout of laughter. Oh, she was magnificent. He had to have her as a lover. But not just yet. He'd sneak up on her till she thought the whole plan had been her idea in the first place. Forget London, Gemma Melcombe would be his greatest conquest.

"Gemma?"

"What?" Her eyes were blazing. Her fangs were bared. Her hands curled into claws that were moments away from scratching his eyes out. And she could, he had no doubt.

"I'm not going to kill Rene."

Oh, he loved throwing her off-balance. She actually took a small step back. "You're not?"

"I only want one thing." He slowly walked around

the desk so that he was standing beside her. He was close enough to feel the warm hum of her skin. He even thought he saw her heart pulse once in the ivory skin of her neck.

"What do you want?" Her voice had dropped. Rough with anger and... desire? Just a hint, but it was there. He'd take it.

"A kiss."

"You want a kiss?"

"One kiss from you, and the boy goes free."

She slid a predatory gaze upward. "One kiss and Rene comes with me tonight? One kiss is all?"

"That's all." He was starting to regret this. One kiss wouldn't be nearly enough.

"Fine." Without warning, she rose and gave him a quick peck on the cheek. "Where's Rene?"

He grinned as he slid an arm around her waist, pulling her into his chest as his mouth slowly descended. "That's not a kiss, luv."

As their lips met, a spark lit the air between them. Water and earth didn't meet with a clash. His amnis slowly lapped up her skin, teasing and testing as his hands pulled her closer. Terry's fangs descended, and he ran his tongue along her lower lip, begging for entry.

Gemma hesitated for only a moment before she gave in. Her lips softened. Her hands gripped the blood-stained collar of his jacket. He knew she could pull away at any moment. Knew her power eclipsed his. The fact that she didn't was intoxicating.

She was so warm. He pulled away for only a second to fill his nose with the scent of her. Roses and jasmine. The earthy smell of fresh rain on grass. She smelled of all that and more. The rigid set of her shoulders relaxed as he held her. Her mouth was as greedy as his, and he groaned into it. She was clean and beautiful and light. She was—

"Enough!"

Gemma pushed him away with a sudden shove. Terry stepped back, as unbalanced as she appeared to be. That had been… far more than a kiss.

"Gemma." His voice sounded like he'd been smoking all night.

"That's enough. Where's Rene?"

"That's enough?" He gave a low chuckle. "That wasn't nearly enough."

"It was enough for our deal. I want my nephew."

Terry eyed her for a moment, then nodded. "Roger?"

His lieutenant stepped through the door. "Yes, boss?"

"Take Ms. Melcombe to Mr. Dupont. He will be released into her custody before he leaves England."

Roger nodded, then Terry spoke to Gemma. "He's not welcome back. If I hear word of him in England while I rule here, I'll kill him, Gemma. See to it he understands. He doesn't get another chance."

She nodded, all business. "Understood."

"And give my respects to your father. His unreserved support is greatly appreciated by Francis Winthrop's successor."

Her eyes turned cold again, and she strode from the room. Terry let her go without another word. Let her take her brother's boy back to him. Let her set up house again in his city. Let her slowly lower her guard. He'd be waiting. He'd be patient. After all, he had the time. And what he'd said to her was true. One kiss wasn't nearly enough.

"Cassiopeia."

"Where?"

"Just there, see?" She held out her finger, tracing the jagged line that crossed the northern sky. "The folds of her dress. Back and forth."

"I liked your wedding dress. Did I tell you that?" They were laying on the deck of the Conquest, spotting constellations. She was far better than he'd thought she'd be, but then, she'd had more than enough time to study. He'd pulled off out every cushion from the boat's cabin, thrown them into a pile, and pulled her down to lie next to him.

"Thank you, but I didn't pick my dress out. The designer did."

He reached over and chuffed her under the chin. "Unsentimental girl, Gem. It's a good thing there was a photographer there. I'd like a proper picture of you in it."

"Just make sure we have every negative, Terry. Every single one. Digital files, too."

"You worry too much. And you've already told Mina. She'll take care of it." He paused and pointed. "Orion."

"The hunter. Friend of the moon-goddess." She pointed again. "Draco."

"Where?"

"Right there, silly." She scooted closer. "See? The long snaking—"

"I'll show you something long and snaking."

She burst into laughter, bumping her forehead against his shoulder. "So mature."

"I try. Show me more."

"Ursa minor. Andromeda."

"I wasn't talking about stars, woman."

"Haha. You have a one track mind. There's Perseus."

Terry smiled. "You know them all, don't you?"

"Yes. And all the stories that go with them. The stars don't change much. It's the same sky I saw when I was a human. Odd, really. Everything else changes." She'd been subdued since he'd risen that night, purposefully keeping their conversations light. They were approaching their home in Spain with every passing night, and Terry hoped he would have enough time.

"Did you ever go to school?"

She shook her head with a frown. "Not as a human. Later of course. Much later. I studied at the Sorbonne shortly before we met. Do you remember? I'd been in Paris. It was because of the university."

He laughed. "Why?"

She shrugged, looking strangely bashful. "Just because I could, I suppose. Ioan thought I was silly, too. But I liked it. Liked being around all the girls who were so young. So alive. It reminded me of... the past, I suppose. I haven't been that young or naive in so long."

"Wise." He reached over, tracing a finger along the arch of her eyebrow. "My wife is wise. I prefer that to naive."

"Terry..."

It was working. Slowly but surely, the water was sloughing off the rocky wall she'd built around her heart. He tried not to be impatient.

"Do you remember the first time you kissed me?"

"Right after you'd taken London? Isn't that the first time *you* kissed *me*?"

"You kissed me back. You were exactly what I needed to see that night. Pulled me back from the edge, I think."

"You were so angry."

He reached over and picked up her hand, weaving their fingers together. "Angry, yes. Grieving. A bit mad with grief, I think. I lost Francis and my brother in the same night."

Gemma's thumb stroked the back of his hand. This was the piece of them that no one else saw. The little moments they'd shared for years that had made him fall in love with her. She was a caretaker at heart, his Gemma. She had a need to care for others that few understood. If she had to bash heads and kill to do it... well, that just made her an excellent vampire.

"You thinking about your brother?"

She gave a sharp nod and he pulled her closer, silently begging to let him give her comfort. He had that night. The night they had killed her brother's murderers she'd come to him, full of rage and grief. He'd loved her as she'd needed it. Wild and fierce to remind herself she was alive. Then slow and quiet, to remind himself that she was safe. That she was his.

"Terry?" Her words were muffled against his chest.

"Hmm?"

"Do you—" She hesitated. "Do you love me?"

He let out a slow breath, cursing his luck. He wouldn't lie to her. He couldn't. It wouldn't be fair to either of them.

"Fuck."

"Do you?"

"Yes."

CHAPTER SIX

He loved her.

Terry loved her.

He didn't sound happy about it, but then she could hardly blame him. She hadn't planned for this.

She had never planned for Terry. In her centuries of life, he was the one person Gemma had never managed to fit into any box. The one who had never behaved as she predicted. A more infuriating, stubborn, arrogant partner she couldn't have found in all the world. And he loved her.

His voice was rough when he finally spoke. "Listen, Gem—"

"I'm horribly afraid of the ocean." She lay in his arms, frozen by her admission. "I know it's not rational, but when I'm on land, everything makes sense. In the ocean, nothing does."

He paused for a moment, then said softly, "You know it can't hurt you."

"I do know that. Rationally, I know that. It's not logical. Father thinks I had an accident when I was human. There's much about my human years I simply don't remember. But I remember the earth. From the first night I woke, I remember feeling it beneath me. The life. The strength. It was..."

"Security?"

"It was everything. To this day, I could be walking through Piccadilly, but I still feel it. Not as strong, perhaps, but there. Always. That quiet hum in my bones. It's everything. Security, yes. Strength. Power."

"But on water—"

"I'm cut off. Imagine floating above the earth with no tether."

"Adrift."

She gave a tight nod. "Yes. Smothered and empty, all at the same time."

They lay silent for a few more minutes, still holding hands and staring up into the night sky. She tried to imagine what expression he wore. Would he be angry? Disappointed? When he finally nudged her to the side, his face was very carefully blank. Not angry, not triumphant at her admission of weakness. Certainly not concerned.

"You know..." He propped his head up in his hand and played with a piece of her hair. For some reason, the familiar habit soothed her. "It's still there, Gem. The earth. It's still under the water."

She broke in. "I know. Rivers don't really bother me. Or lakes. But the ocean—"

"It's still there, luv. Underneath all the sea, the earth remains, just as it's always been. It's what the water rests on, isn't it?" He leaned over and gently kissed her forehead. "You're thinking of it all wrong. The ocean flows over the earth, it doesn't smother it."

She took a deep, unnecessary breath to calm herself. "I know."

"And the sand drifts through it. Volcanos press up. The earth... it's what shapes the water. Gives it direction."

Gemma felt unexpected tears come to the corner of her eyes. She cleared her throat. "You're a poet, Terry."

"Want me to curse again? Just to make you feel better?" He pinched her waist teasingly. "Bugger the ocean. You're tougher than a great drink of water."

She couldn't hold in the laugh.

"Stiff upper lip, old girl. What would the Queen say?"

She punched him. "Shut up."

Now he was laughing, too. "Dammit, Gemma, are you an Englishwoman or not? You live on a great, bloody island after all. Do your ancestors proud!"

"You're crazy."

He grabbed her and pulled her in for a quick, heart-thumping kiss. "Aye. I am. For lots of reasons."

Like loving me.

"Listen... Terry—"

"Come on." He was already standing, holding out his hand. "Let's go."

"Where?" She took it, and he pulled her to her feet.

"For a swim."

Gemma dug in her heels the instant he pulled harder. "No."

"Yes." He stopped and turned to her. "Do you trust me?"

Did she? Yes. However complicated her feelings for Terry might have been, she did trust him.

She was still hesitating when he said, "You've never run from anything in your life. Don't be a coward, Gemma Melcombe."

Well, that did it. She couldn't back down now. Terry challenging her was the surest way to make her stubborn about something, and he knew it. He did it just to be contrary at times.

"Fine," she muttered.

"What?"

"You heard me." She punched his arm, but he only smiled. "Where are we going?"

He held up a finger, then stripped all his clothes off before he dove in. He surfaced and said, "I have an idea." Then he was gone again.

One minute.

Two.

Five.

She knew not to be nervous. Knew it. He was in his element for God's—

She heard the water break. "Terry?"

"Here," he laughed, pulling himself up the ladder to peek over the edge. "Just here. Unfortunately, there's not much out there. I'll take you to warmer waters some day and swim in the reefs, but I did find something fun."

She bit her lip. "What is it?"

"A surprise. I'll not let anything happen. I promise."

"Are there sharks?"

He burst into laughter. "You can't be afraid of sharks."

"I told you it wasn't rational!"

Terry was still laughing when he climbed dripping over the side of the Conquest. "Take off your clothes and get in the water."

She hesitated.

He gave her a warning look. "Gemma..."

"Fine." She pulled at her bikini top. Wherever they were sailing, the nights had slowly become balmy, so the air temperature was more than comfortable. Still, Terry eyed her breasts and they came to attention. Infuriating man. Her body always had a mind of its own when it came to him.

"You know, on second thought—"

She cut him off by diving into the water, surfacing to see him watching her with hungry eyes.

"Is there anything good to eat in here? I'm getting sick of the preserved blood." She slicked the hair back from her face and deliberately kept from squirming at the overwhelming sensation of emptiness that surrounded her. Plus, the air may have been warm, but the water was still the Atlantic. It was more than a little chilly.

"Sharks." Terry dove in, swimming underneath her, then sliding up her back and letting his hands run over every curve on the way up. Suddenly, the feeling of emptiness was gone and he was there; his amnis wrapped around her like a blanket as his mouth kissed the curve of her neck. "But then I tend to find the most vicious things delicious."

He hadn't let go of her hand once. Gemma swam through the dark sea, finally becoming accustomed to the water that filled her unmoving lungs. Once she had overcome her initial panic, she discovered Terry was right. Allowing the water to fill her airways was far more comfortable than trying to hold breath that didn't need to be held. First they were under for only a few minutes. Then a few more, but the longer Gemma stayed beneath the surface, holding Terry's hand, the more comfortable she became. He didn't push her, allowing her to swim at her own pace as they slowly moved farther away from the boat.

Despite the cold Northern waters, life was everywhere. The ocean teemed with it. Fish darted away from them in massive silver schools. Sharks, which panicked her at first, fled from them instinctually. Terry had only smiled. From one predator to another, it seemed that the sharks knew what was best for them.

Finally, she pulled him up to the surface and coughed the water from her throat, trying not to gag.

"What—" Cough. "—were you trying to surprise me with again?"

He ran gentle fingers through her hair, tucking the wet strands back behind her ears as he looked around. "They've moved off. I suppose it was odd to see them here anyway. They're usually much deeper."

"What are you talking about?"

Just then, a tiny light caught her eye. Then another. And another. The moon was full, but the seas were completely dark, except for the tiny rainbow flashes. She looked to her husband, who was grinning.

"Moonjellys."

"What?" She pulled him closer. "Jellyfish?"

"Not exactly. No stingers on these little beauties. They're not jellyfish, just called moonjellys." His hand passed near one, which lit up with tiny lights and moved away. "These fellows are usually drifting far deeper. Caught them earlier tonight and I wanted to show you." He continued to move through the water, pulling her behind him and every nudge of the water lit up more of the tiny creatures. They rippled and pulsed in the water, flowing around them in glowing currents.

"They're beautiful. Like stars in the water."

"They light up if you get close, spread your hand out."

She did and laughed when she saw the tiny riots of color.

"I've never seen a mass of them like this," he said. "No idea what's going on. Maybe they just wanted to say hello."

Gemma looked down till her nose was almost in the water. "Hello back, ocean."

Without warning, she was enveloped in a tight embrace. Terry wrapped his arms around her and she felt his amnis call to the water around them, holding their bodies buoyant as he swept her into a joyful kiss. She could feel the smile on his lips when he pressed them to her lips, her cheeks, her forehead. He was boyish in his affection. Gemma couldn't help but smile back.

"Thank you," he said as he smiled. "Thank you for coming with me."

"As long... well, as long as you hold my hand, I feel safe."

"Then I'll never let it go." He smiled again and tugged her back toward where the boat must have been. "At least not off shore."

"That's highly impractical."

"I don't care."

"Really Terry—"

He dove at her, wrapping her in his arms as they plunged beneath the water and he took her breath away with his lips. Terry rolled in the waves, spinning her in the cloud of moonjellys as they lit up the dark water and surrounded them with tiny rainbows.

He loves me.

He loves me.

He loves me, too...

She broke away with a gasp as they surfaced. *Too*?

Did she love Terry? What did love even mean to someone as old as she was? Was she even capable of it anymore?

She felt a sudden ache in her chest and blinked away tears.

"Gem?"

"Can we go back to the boat?"

"Too much." He frowned. "Sorry. This is too much, isn't it?"

"I'm fine. I'm just... it's all a bit overwhelming."

"Of course." He wrapped an arm around her waist and pulled Gemma up on his chest as he lay back in the water. "Relax now. Let me show off a bit. I'll have us back in no time."

"Really?" He sped off, but she would have sworn he didn't move at all. There was no kicking. No effort. Terry simply moved through the ocean, cradling Gemma on his broad chest and stroking her back. She finally relaxed and tucked her head under his chin to enjoy the ride.

"Did you have fun?" he asked.

"Surprisingly yes."

"We'll go someplace warmer and explore a reef someday. The cold water doesn't produce the brilliant colors. The Tropics are fun."

"Is that why you're always trying to convince me to go to the Bahamas?"

"That and tiny swimsuits, luv." He reached down and gave her ass a pinch. "Can't forget those."

"Of course not."

It was getting close to dawn, so they headed directly to their secured room under the boat. For the first time, entering the small outer hatch did not fill Gemma with dread. She simply closed her eyes and pressed her face into Terry's chest until she could feel the air surrounding them. They both grabbed towels to dry themselves, neither bothering with clothes. They were both more than comfortable in their skins.

Gemma studied him as he readied the room, making sure the heater was turned on for her. She knew the cold didn't bother him, but she was on the warmer end of the vampire spectrum, so cold did cause discomfort. He tossed another pillow on the low bed, then straightened the linens and grabbed another blanket from a built in chest.

"Do you want some blood before dawn?" he asked.

"No, thank you." She didn't really have to feed more than once every two weeks or so. Terry had to drink more.

She kept watching him, suddenly aware of his presence in a way she hadn't been in years. His body was built for strength, with muscular legs and a trim waist. Broad shoulders that would never stoop with age or lose their strength. Terry ran a quick hand over the hair he'd always kept trimmed unfashionably short. He moved quickly, efficient in every movement; his eyes darted around the room, instinctually checking for any weakness or danger. It was the way he had always been.

Her husband wasn't made for fine rooms and tailored suits. He had a body built for violence and the mind of a conman. It was exactly those qualities that had made his sire turn him. It was part of the reason she'd chosen him as her husband. And now he was hers.

Gemma's eyes were drawn to the curve of muscle where his neck met his shoulder.

"Have you ever shared blood with anyone, Terry?"

He froze, his back to her. "No."

"Oh."

He paused. "Have you?"

"I..." She had dreamed about sharing that bond with her human husband, but it hadn't been possible. And she had taken his vein, but not often. He hadn't enjoyed it. William had never been totally at ease with the creature she was. "No," she said. "I haven't."

A heavy silence lay between them. He still had his back to her, tension evident in his shoulders.

"You know I'd never deny you anything in my power to give you, Gemma," he said in a low voice. "But if you want something, you'll have to ask. I'm done offering."

Her fangs ran down when she heard his heart thump. He wanted her to bite him, wanted that intimacy between them. Her skin prickled in awareness, and Gemma realized she wanted him to bite her, too. She wanted it so badly her fangs ached in her mouth.

Too much! Her mind rebelled.

She rose and went to him, wrapping her arms around him from behind, reveling the smooth expanse of his back under her mouth. She kissed along his spine as her hands splayed along his belly. For once, she wanted to be slow. She wanted to appreciate each moment with him. Gemma pressed her ear to his back, listening to the slow thump of his excited heart as his hands covered hers, holding her close.

"My Gemma," he whispered.

Your Gemma.

She could give him that. Maybe she was no longer capable of love. She probably didn't deserve her husband's. But if Terry wanted her, she could be his.

His energy reached out to the water that dotted her skin, fluttering over her body with tiny vibrations that caused her to gasp in pleasure. His amnis licked at her though not a single muscle flinched. Gemma closed her eyes and drunk it in. It was familiar and new all at once. The feel of his body under her hands. The same smell in her nose. The taste of his skin. The overwhelming raw energy of their touch ignited every nerve in her body.

For over fifteen years they had been lovers, and it had always been this way. Terry was her own familiar mystery. Each time she thought she had the puzzle solved, new pieces were thrown at her. She opened her eyes and saw the luxurious linens he'd brought onto the boat for her. The Egyptian cotton towels in the chest. The low whir of the heater that cut the natural chill of the water. For her.

"My husband takes good care of me," she murmured.

She heard him give a low laugh. "He'd hear it if he didn't."

Gemma ducked under his arm and moved in front of him, drawing him down to the bed, covering herself with the solid feel of his body over hers. She pressed a lingering kiss to his lips. "I don't need to be taken care of," she murmured against his lips. "But I find that I do enjoy it."

The corner of his mouth turned up in a crooked

smile. "Good. I don't plan on stopping anytime soon."

She gently pushed his shoulders back and rolled on top, kissing down his chest as she slid onto him. He arched up in pleasure, groaning out her name. Gemma closed her eyes and focused on the familiar push and pull of their bodies together, memorizing his breath, pressing his hands closer when they stroked over her favorite spots.

Gemma tortured them both with slow pleasure, touching the edge over and over, only to pull back and focus on her lover until he grew mad with her teasing. Finally losing patience, Terry sat up, grabbing the hair at the nape of her neck and pulling her in for a bruising kiss as he took control.

"My turn, luv."

Her breath caught as he drove them harder. He tugged her hair again, forcing her eyes to his.

"I want to see you."

"Terry..."

"Gemma." He breathed out her name like a prayer and she felt her body coiling with tension, seconds away from breaking free. She couldn't take her eyes from him. His mouth was set in a stubborn line as he drove her to the edge of release. Closer. Closer... Suddenly, his lips softened as he whispered, "I love you, Gemma."

She shattered.

CHAPTER SEVEN

"Terry." He was groggy from his day rest when he heard her voice. "Terry."

He reached for her instinctively, only to feel her grab his wrist and bend it back. He frowned, his eyes still closed.

"Terry." Her quiet voice was a little more urgent.

"Early, luv," he mumbled.

"I knew this was going to be a problem with a younger man."

"I 'ave to be..." He somehow managed to shake off the ache in his wrist and pull Gemma closer. "Keep up with you."

"You're not making sense. And you need to wake up now."

"No." He was comfortable. And Gemma was right next to him where she belonged. "Why... don' you share my room when we get home, Gem? Be nice, you know..."

"Terrance, wake up. There are five humans and two vampires on this vessel."

Th-thunk. His heart gave a quick lurch and he opened his eyes. *Th-thunk.*

He held out his hand. "Blood. Now." He felt her put the cold packet in his hand and he brought it to his mouth, biting through the plastic and draining it quickly. He sat up. Gemma was wearing a pair of black leggings and a bikini top.

"What else do you need to wake up?"

Terry dragged her mouth to his, nicking her bottom lip with his fang and sucking hard as she let out a barely audible whimper.

"Terry—"

"More later." He could feel the heady energy filling him. It was more than the few drops he'd tasted by accident in the past. He'd taken a solid swallow of Gemma's powerful blood and could already feel the effects. His limbs prickled with awareness, the fog began to lift from his mind, and his senses went on alert. He was also hard as a rock, but there wasn't much he could do about that. Damn.

"The humans arrived during the daylight, but obviously, I couldn't do much. The two vampires just arrived."

"Any sense of them?"

"Not much. I don't recognize any voices. The humans have been bashing around in the back of the stateroom for over an hour." As if to demonstrate, Terry heard a solid thump on the other side of the wall separating the day chamber from the interior cabin.

"Bloody humans on my boat," he muttered, curling his lip. "Fucking vampires. Kill every last one of them, just for disturbing my honeymoon. Dammit, Gem. Can we get a single week to ourselves?"

She was looking around the wooden chamber of the Conquest with wide eyes. "There's only one way out of this chamber. I don't like this."

"They'd have to have a battering ram to get in."

"How did they find us? I thought you said that Carl

and Roger were the only ones who knew about this boat."

He felt his brain pick up her train of thought. The realization brought a pang of unexpected grief. "Then Carl is dead."

"Roger?"

"Not likely. Carl was human. We have to assume it was Carl." Amnis or torture? It could be either, but for his assistant's sake, he hoped it was the former. Terry pushed a button in the wall and heard the hiss of the pneumatics as the wooden panel lifted to reveal a few small monitors. He squinted, making sure not to get too close so he didn't short out the equipment.

"I know that one." Gemma pointed to one monitor, which immediately went fuzzy. Terry batted her hand away.

"Look, don't touch. Which one? The shorter one?" He glanced at the humans; two were stumbling around on deck and the other three were still searching the cabin for some kind of trap door.

"Yes." She glanced at him from the corner of her eye. "He's Leonor's."

A cold knot settled in his stomach. "You're sure?" The Spanish noblewoman was almost as old as Gemma and known to be as ruthless as Terry. She'd controlled the Iberian peninsula and the Straight of Gibraltar through more regimes than Terry could count. She was not only powerful, but rich. All trade into the Mediterranean passed through her shipping lanes, owing her tribute. Leonor was a formidable opponent who he would have bet with confidence was an ally.

"Let's not jump to conclusions," Gemma said, as if

reading his mind. "This would be foolish of her. Why get rid of us? She doesn't have the physical resources to take London, nor the ambition. This could be an internal problem that we were dragged into."

"Or it could have to do with that bloody elixir, Gem."

"Or that."

They watched for a few more minutes. The two vampires were conferring on the deck. One grabbed a bottle of the blood wine from the cabinet, eyeing it with interest.

"Damn," he muttered. "If he wasn't dead before, he is now." Terry wasn't willing to let them have their business secrets any more than the personal ones.

"Plan?"

"Did you hear any boats?"

"No."

"Then it's likely humans brought them during the day while you were sleeping. Has to be at least one boat. Maybe more. No telling how many humans aboard."

"They wouldn't want to attract attention."

Terry shrugged and stood up, debating whether to put on clothes. "It's a big ocean. And we're out in the middle of it." With a grimace, he settled on a pair of black swim shorts. He may not have liked wearing clothes in the water, but neither did he plan on killing and maiming with his glory flapping in the breeze.

"Ah yes, out in the middle of the Atlantic. Have I told you what an excellent plan that was, darling?"

Terry grinned. She'd never called him 'darling' before. "Just look on the bright side, luv. No one will raise any questions when they hear the screams, now will they?"

"True," she said just as he heard the splash. His eyes darted back to the monitor. Only one vampire was visible on the screens. "Vampire overboard."

"He cannot find this chamber." Terry's eyes locked on Gemma's. "If it's compromised, we'll have to reach land by dawn or rest very, very deep."

He saw the battle lust fill her eyes and her fangs run out in her mouth. "Ready?" he asked.

"Of course." She went to him eagerly, wrapping her arms around his waist as he opened the trap door and lay down in the narrow chamber. Her energy was jumping and he could feel the blood churning in her normally slow veins. "You're excited about killing something, aren't you?"

Gemma smiled, her fangs gleaming behind her rosebud lips. "I don't like being bored."

"No, you don't." He punched the button and let the hydraulic lever go to work, sealing them in, then the outer door released, flooding the small chamber with water.

Ah, yes. His amnis reached out, immediately identifying the other immortal nearby. The door opened. With a quick twist, he shoved Gemma from his arms and she slipped under the keel to the opposite side of the Conquest. He spun to block the dagger that had been coming at his throat, twisting around, trying to lock his legs around his attacker to immobilize him.

No good. His opponent was a water vamp, just like him. The force of the current buffeted him before he could block it, then Terry heard a scraping sound and a splash as another body entered the water.

Terry couldn't tell where it came from, and he had

no time to look. He had to trust that Gemma would have enough control underwater that she could handle herself. The vampire had not stopped attacking, and Terry had no knife. He kept weapons, but none in his day chamber.

The immortal attacking him had dusky skin and long hair that kept drifting into his eyes as the water swirled around them. Terry bared his fangs. Amateur.

Not spending enough time in your element, are you?

Terry dove, darting deep into the black water, and he heard his opponent follow. The other man felt older than him in years, but he did not have the elemental control that Terry did. He let his amnis flow, reaching out with the current until he felt the thin thread of the other vampire's energy. He tugged, but the man was still swimming in circles, trying to see him.

Foolish vampire.

Terry didn't need to see him, his amnis already did. He carefully surrounded the vampire with coils of energy, wrapping him with ribbons of water invisible to the other man. Then, he pulled.

In the blink of an eye, the liquid ribbons turned to steel, constricting the other vampire and stilling his arms as the knife slipped from his fingers. Terry's amnis scooped it up, bringing the knife to his palm as he grabbed the other man by his mop of dark hair.

He searched for her, following the chaotic sounds of splashing to the other boat, whose dark hull lay fifty meters away. As he approached, he sensed them.

Tricky girl. Terry grinned. Looked like someone was making new friends.

His arm darted out and caught the fin as it tried to slip past. The mako was quick, but not as quick as he was. Still, it whipped around, almost slashing Terry's arm before his hand brushed along the head, stroking the nose and letting his amnis reach out until the great animal calmed. The smell of human blood was heady in the water, which must have drawn the sharks. Terry reached out and petted it, the other vampire still struggling under his control, until he saw her.

She was feasting on the neck of a struggling human, the blood a cloud around her that the sharks circled with excitement. He moved closer, careful not to startle her out of her bloodlust. She saw him from the corner of her eye and pushed the limp body away, swimming toward him, fangs bared and hair streaming in the moonlit water. She grabbed him by the neck and pulled his mouth to hers, biting on his lower lip and sucking hard as she pushed them to the surface.

Gemma threw her head back as they breached the water, and Terry immediately slapped a hand over her mouth so she didn't make a sound. She bit his finger, but didn't speak. Terry held his finger up to his lips and she nodded. Then he motioned to the struggling captive, who he was still holding with one hand.

"Recognize him?"

"No," she whispered. "The other must still be on the Conquest. We only need one alive."

He nodded, then made quick work of his extra cargo before the words could register with the other vampire, slicing around his neck with the man's own dagger, spilling his blood and severing his spine before he let the limp body sink. Then he grabbed Gemma with both hands, cupping her cheeks and licking at the trickle of blood that leaked down her chin from her split lip. Their lips met, bruising and hungry as their energy crashed together. Terry used the water to push her closer, overcome by need for her. Her blood called to him, spurred on by the hunt as his body answered her. Finally, he broke away with a gasp.

"Gemma!"

"We can't. Not here. Not like this."

He nodded, gritting his teeth as his fangs pierced his lower lip and his blood dropped into the churning water.

"Soon," he growled.

She was panting. Her lips swollen with lust and her cheeks flushed with blood. "Soon."

A sleek fin surfaced only meters away, then disappeared under the waves.

"They shy away from us," she said in wonder. "But if you touch them—"

"It's their electroreceptors." He motioned to the calm mako, who was still circling Terry as if fascinated. "Hundreds of them. In their head, mostly. It's partly how they sense prey in the water."

"And why they keep away from us."

"Amnis is electricity, luv. They sense it almost as well as we do."

"But they don't have a shield. They're like humans that way."

"That's right." He reached out for the shark, who rubbed up against his arm like a cat. "Give their nose a pat, and they're friendly as a pup."

"Amazing." A smile broke over her face. "It's amazing."

Terry winked. "Ocean's not so bad, is it? Now, how many?" The shouts from the boats were finally reaching his ears, Spanish voices yelling to find them. Calling for missing comrades.

"There were only humans on the other boat. Three. I grabbed one and pulled him in. Used his blood to attract the sharks. That made the other two panic. They were easy to grab. I drank from one and left the other to the... puppies."

"Very considerate. So we have one other vampire and five humans on the Conquest."

She nodded. "But we need the vampire alive if we want to question him."

"Aye. So"—He cocked his head toward the boat. "—do you want the humans or the vampire?"

"You take the humans," she said with a wicked smile. "You're going to need the energy soon."

Sometimes, there really wasn't anything more satisfying than bashing a few heads in. When one belonged to the earth vampire who had interrupted your honeymoon, it was particularly gratifying.

"Who else?" Gemma calmly asked as Terry took another swing.

"Th-that's all. It was only her. Leonor sent us."

"I think you're lying, Gaston."

"She wants Ramsay out of power! Leonor thinks he's going to ally with Jean Desmarais in France and take Spain so they can both avoid the Gibraltar tariffs."

"Avoiding taxes?" Terry paused, a frown marking his face. "Desmarais and I are going to throw over an ally to save a bit of gold? You expect me to believe Leonor thinks I'm stupid enough to do that?"

The Spaniard actually managed a condescending expression, which Terry took as his cue to hit him again. There was a satisfying crunch when his fist landed.

Gemma sat up straighter. "Did you break your hand, darling?"

"No, luv. Give him a minute. Think I might have dislocated his jaw on that one."

As the other man sat groaning, Gemma slipped to Terry's side, speaking quietly in Welsh. The language was rarely spoken on the Continent, which was handy.

"They were expected to fail," she said.

"I can't deny that I'm enjoying the interrogation, but I think he may be telling the truth."

"He believes what he's been told, but I think you're right."

"You don't really think Leonor—"

"Of course not." She tapped her chin. "But someone sent these men here, along with the humans, to fail. We capture them. Question them—"

"And they spill about Leonor. It's false, of course—"

Gemma nodded. "But they want to plant the seed of doubt."

"Combine this with the smuggling problems her envoy came to talk about..."

"She's being felt out."

Terry said, "Just like Murphy in Dublin."

"And the Dutch. The bankers have been quiet about it, but Guy mentioned some problems to me at the reception."

Terry took a step back, staring out over the water, something about the whole situation tickling the back of his mind.

Spain, Marseilles, Dublin, the Netherlands.

"What am I not seeing?" he muttered.

"The sun?" the bound Spaniard sneered. "The sky is already growing light, you fool. Are you going to kill me or not? If not, I'd prefer to find shelter."

Terry ignored him and looked over at Gemma, who appeared to be studying her manicure. "All right, luv?"

"I chipped a fingernail. It must have been when I was feeding the sharks. How annoying."

"There there," he chuckled. "You poor thing."

"Don't jest, Terry. My nails take ages to grow."

"What shall we do with the good *señor*, wife?"

She looked over the edge of the boat. "Do sharks like vampire meat?"

He saw their captive still. "'Fraid not. Blood doesn't pump quite hot enough for them."

"Gaston?" She rose and walked to the Spaniard. "Who killed Carl?"

The vampire's fangs ran down. "Killed who?"

"Carl. My husband's human secretary. I can tell by your reaction you're remembering a recent kill." Gemma's blue eyes turned icy. "It's so hard to hide sometimes, isn't it? The memory of their blood hot in your mouth, that slow thud as their heart stops." She stared into the vampire's brown eyes. "Did he cry out? Scream for mercy?"

Gaston's lip curled when he answered, "No."

"Did you torture him?"

Terry snarled when the man remained silent. One

look from Gemma told him she was as furious as he was.

"It's too bad that Terry killed your friend, Gaston. You see, we share everything, and that makes you mine." Gemma leaned down, raking her fingernails along Gaston's cheek. "And I liked Carl Stanton. Which means you will not die quickly. I might break another nail, but somehow, I think it will be worth it."

CHAPTER EIGHT

Gemma forced her eyes open most of the day. She was over eight hundred years old, but still had to sleep for a few hours. Despite the extermination of the boarding party and the elimination of the threat, she felt exposed. She was accustomed to being in more familiar surroundings, paranoid about security, and vigilant about who she trusted. Currently, the vampire in her arms topped the list.

Terrance Ramsay. Who would have thought they would come to this? He was supposed to be her partner. She'd always enjoyed him as a lover. But this...

She remembered the previous night, watching him as he twisted in the water, bending it to his will as he killed their attacker. Shoving her out of the way, yet trusting her to protect herself. Trusting her to defend him as he had defended her. He really and truly was her partner.

She did love him.

How completely unexpected. How *beautiful*.

Gemma felt a tear well at the corner of her eye and wondered what, exactly, she had done to deserve that kind of gift after so many hundreds of years. It was only a hint now, only the promise of what could be, that curled in her chest. She knew with time, it could become quite overwhelming. She had loved her human husband passionately, but he had never been her equal, not as Terry was.

"'Let me not to the marriage of true minds admit impediments,'" she whispered the old words of Shakespeare's sonnet to him as he slumbered. "'Love is not love which alters when it alteration finds, or bends with the remover to remove: O no! it is an ever-fixed mark...'"

"'—that looks on tempests and is never shaken.'" His quiet voice surprised her as he continued the lines. "'It is the star to every wandering bark, whose worth's unknown, although his height be taken.'" Slowly, Terry's eyes blinked open. "Good evening, Gem."

She could feel her heart beating when she asked, "Why do you love me?"

"For that."

"Pardon?"

"Your honesty. Your directness. You can play games —I've seen you twist around the wiliest vampire with your charm—but you don't. Not with me. You never have. If anything, you've been rude and abrupt."

"You like it?"

"I do." He smiled. "I like knowing you trust me enough to show me the real Gemma, not the diplomat or the flirt. I love that you're honest with me. I love that you're one of the most loyal daughters I've ever met. And sisters. You'd raze the city if you thought one of your loved ones was in danger. You'd skewer anyone who threatened them without a thought to what it might cost you."

"That's not true. I always take safety considerations into mind. I'm not very much use to anyone if I'm dead, are I?"

He pulled her closer, tucking her blond head under his chin. "You're funny and smart and fierce. And you don't take any shit from me."

"You have your own kind of charm, Terry. And your men adore you. Someone has to keep you in line."

"That's why I married you."

Gemma felt an unexpected twist in her chest. "That's why?"

She felt his finger under her chin, pressing up until their eyes met. "Well, that. And the fact that I'm truly..." Terry pressed a kiss to her forehead. "Utterly..." Another along her cheekbone. "...mad about you." His lips met hers, spinning her out until she felt wrapped in tiny threads of his amnis. Surrounded. Enthralled. She'd never been drunk as a human, but she imagined it must have felt like kissing Terry. He took her mouth in tiny bites that teased her, always leaving her wanting more. She tried to tug him closer. More. He rolled over her, working his mouth down her neck, over the taut peaks of her breasts, past the quivering skin of her belly.

"You drive me mad, Gem." His lips and tongue touched. Tasted. She could feel his fangs tease the inside of her thigh.

"Terry—"

"I thought—" He was practically vibrating with need. His voice scraped along her skin. "—I could control it. Thought I could play the part."

"You don't—"

"I can't!" His fingers gripped her hips, lifting her body to his mouth so he could feast. "I'll have all of you. Do you understand? All of you. Till I live in your blood."

"Terry!" she sobbed, teetering on the edge, mad with desire and drunk from his words. "I love you."

He stilled. Every nerve in her body jumped as his body stilled and his amnis swept over her. What had been a gentle lapping turned into a roaring wave. Desire. Joy. Every hair on her body rose with his touch.

"Come again."

"I almost was." Before she could blink, he was over her, braced on steel arms, inches from her face, and clearly not in a joking mood.

"Again."

Gemma traced the hard planes of his face, running her hands over the hint of stubble that covered his jaw. Then she looked into his eyes and said, "I love you."

He said nothing. Terry was frozen. In shock? She began to fidget. "I'm not sure I know how to love someone, to be totally honest. I'm really very old. And... the one time I tried long ago, it didn't work. But he was human, and you're..." Why was she talking about this? This wasn't what she wanted to say. Not truly. "I love you, Terry. I think I have for some time, I just didn't realize it. But it's you. And you know me... probably better than anyone. You understand me. And you say you love me anyway, so—"

"I do love you," he finally spoke. "I just couldn't imagine what it would feel like if you felt the same."

She glanced away from his penetrating stare. "And what does it feel like?"

"More," he whispered. "More than I imagined."

And he was there again, placing gentle kisses along her face, whispering sweet words in her ear, flooding her skin with his energy as he joined their bodies. Terry wrapped her legs around his waist before he slid home and eased the ache that had overtaken her. Her body and mind breathed a sigh of relief.

Mate.

Home.

It was right. For the first time in hundreds of years, Gemma hungered for a male in every way. Her body ached for him. Her vampire nature hungered for his blood, and her heart... Her heart was safe in his care. She knew it with certainty.

She gripped his forearms, sliding her hands up to caress the steel-corded muscles of his powerful body. She almost came from the knowledge that soon, her blood would travel within his own. Then, he would truly be hers. She bared her neck to him in a rare show of submission.

"Gemma?" he rasped through the pounding rhythm of their lovemaking.

"Bite me."

He groaned. "Are you sure?"

Was she? A part of her was frightened. Exposed. "Please, just—"

He struck hard and fast.

She gasped, "Oh, sweet heaven. No wonder humans like this so much."

"Oh, Gem," he moaned. He didn't only bite her once. The sharp pleasure-pain was repeated on the other side of her neck, where he latched on and drank in hard pulls. She felt him swell and pulse inside her, the pumping of his heart roaring in her ears. Finally, he let go, only to roll over and push her up so he could pierce the soft underside of her breast with his teeth, all the while thrusting with lazy rhythm as she started to feel the effects.

"Your blood—" He pulled away from her left breast to nuzzle her right, murmuring against her skin. "—is like the finest wine. So sweet. Bloody hell, you're amazing."

"No one..." She could barely speak. Her head was spinning. "No one's ever bitten me before. I never let them."

She heard Terry growl and he bit harder, but it only made her moan in pleasure. She was past climax. She had come every time his teeth punctured her skin, but he had still not spent himself. Her fangs ached in her mouth.

It wasn't pleasure she wanted.

As if reading her mind, Terry finally pulled away, and Gemma leaned in, licking her blood from his lips. Delving into his mouth as he groaned. Stroking his fangs with her tongue. They were still joined, so she took a moment rocking in his embrace, inhaling the scent of him before she tugged his ear, exposing his neck to her eyes.

"Oh yes," he moaned. "Fucking hell, Gem."

She took a moment to appreciate what a fine specimen her mate was. Strong. Virile. A cord of muscle ran up his neck. She nudged his chin up, exposing the soft, vulnerable skin at the base of his throat. He had other such vulnerable places. Another time, she would explore them all. But for now...

"Bite me," he growled. "Now."

"Patience," she purred, licking up the side of his neck. The anticipation was always half the fun.

"I'm out of patien—God yes!"

His blood burst into her mouth. Rich, thick, not sweet. It was heady with the flavor that teased his skin. Redolent with salt and wind and pulsing with life. It filled her mouth and poured down her throat as she drank him in. Gemma grabbed onto him, pressing his neck to her mouth, angling his head back as his body arched in pleasure and he exploded beneath her. His hands were thrown out, bracing himself as she rode him.

It could have been hours or minutes. She lost all concept of time. There was only him. Filling her every sense.

The feel of his skin, so different from her own.

His scent. He smelled of the sea and the cold whipping air that crossed the ocean.

Terry's touch was a riot of sensation. Hard and gripping. Soft and teasing. And she wanted more more more. It would never be enough.

His amnis followed his blood, teasing down her neck, between her breasts, fluttering over her belly before it spread to her limbs. Filling her, surrounding her. Like a single drop of blood in water, he spread and filled every corner. They were one. Joined in every way. Gemma almost wept with the joy of it. She was replete with love.

"I love you," she whispered against his skin, feeling the hot tears slip down her cheeks. "It was more than I could imagine, too."

She pulled away from his neck and Terry sat up straighter, limp with pleasure, but smiling. He cupped her face and brushed the tears from her cheeks, kissing her trembling mouth as he soothed her.

"Oh Gem." He kissed her again, still smiling. "There's my girl. There you are, luv."

She threw her arms around him and let him hold her. "I love you."

"I love you too, wife." Terry stroked her hair and rocked her as she trembled. "It was well worth the wait."

Gemma lay soft and sated in Terry's arms. "I feel very vulnerable on this boat."

"I'll admit, that was the idea. Forgive me, but you can be a bit prickly when we're—"

"No literally. Vulnerable. Our position has been compromised. We sunk the boat and shorted out all the electrical equipment aboard, but the fact remains that someone found us once, and there is no guarantee that whoever it was didn't tell someone else."

"Oh."

They were both silent for a moment.

"So, that was the plan?" she finally asked. "Isolate me and then seduce me over and over until—"

"You enjoyed the seducing part; don't lie."

She couldn't help but smile. "You played me."

"I did."

He was still as a statue, his arms around her tense.

"Well played, sir."

She felt him relax and pull her even closer.

"I figured about a fifty-fifty chance that you'd kill me when you figured it out."

"It's a good thing I love you so much, then."

"A good thing indeed." He laughed and kissed the top of her head. "A very good thing. But you're right. We should make land as quickly as possible."

"We'll have to approach the house with caution. Leonor knows it's ours."

"True."

"So how long to get there?" She stood and began pacing the cabin. She was a bit worried until she saw his expression. "Terry?"

"Eh... I might have been dragging out the journey a bit."

She narrowed her eyes. "How long?"

He glanced at the clock in the cabin. "This little thing isn't hard to move if I just use my amnis... I could have us there an hour or so before dawn."

"What, have we just been going in circles or something?"

His smile turned into a laugh, which turned into a roar. She punched his shoulder.

"You're an ass, Terry."

"But I'm your ass."

"An *ass*! You know I don't like being on the water, but you still—"

He pulled her down and stopped her mouth with a hard kiss. "Well played, remember?"

"And you'll never be able to pull this again."

"I should hope not."

He patted her bum and rose from the soft pallet on the floor. Gemma looked around the room with a bit of sadness. To be completely safe, they'd have to get rid of the boat. Since it had been found once, it could be found again. It wasn't large enough to defend properly and was useless for stealth...

"We'll have another built," Terry said, catching her expression. "If you like, I'll build you a hundred."

She shrugged. "It's hardly necessary. But I do admit a certain fondness for this little room."

"I do, too."

Brushing off her melancholy, she focused on the tasks ahead. "Things in Spain could be quite interesting."

"Since I told Leonor we were coming to negotiate that trade agreement with the Moroccans, I imagine you're right."

She gasped. "Terry! You included some business on our honeymoon?"

"Thought you'd appreciate the multi-tasking."

"You do love me."

"I know my girl." He checked the video feed for the boat one more time before he held out a hand. "Can't have you bored now, can we? Ready for general mayhem, luv?"

"Lead the way."

The voyage to the mainland went quickly, with Gemma hiding inside the main cabin to avoid the stinging winds of the Atlantic as they made their way to the *Rias de Galicia.* The Northwest corner of Spain was marked by numerous jagged "*rias*," deep sheltered bays dug into the granite of the Galician coast. It was an area ruled by the water. Tourists mingled with mussel farmers. Small sun-baked villages butted up to the water and tiny islands dotted many of the rias, making each a world unto itself in many ways. Terry and Gemma had a large house just outside of Muros in the Ria de Muros, one of the larger, warmer rias.

It was an area with little to no regular vampire population, but a surprising number of immortals used the place for meetings. It was convenient to reach from Northern Africa, France, and Spain, so many immortals with shipping interests made their way to negotiate deals or spend "quality time" with their allies.

Ria de Muros was a neutral place—as much as any place was neutral—and had the advantage of beautiful scenery and lively Spanish nightlife. Further, it was well within Leonor's territory. And Leonor was known for fierce fairness.

The only drawback to their home in Muros was that it was known. They had an unassuming safe house outside one of the smaller villages, but their larger home would be watched. Gemma looked with longing toward the lights of the comfortable house that reflected in the water. If anyone had broken in or was laying in wait, she would be very put out.

"There's not enough time tonight," she heard Terry mutter as they drew closer in the small raft he'd inflated to take them to shore. "Not secure, luv, we'll have to stay in the safe house until tomorrow."

"Damn. They better not have touched the household staff."

"They were sent to fail, remember?" He turned the boat around and headed back to the Conquest. "Whoever was sent after us was meant to fail. Which means whoever sent them is expecting us. They also probably know that we know. They'll make their play in the open first. This is Muros. If they're meeting us here, they've come for negotiation."

Despite the late hour, it was tourist season, so the sounds of live music drifted across the small harbor that fronted the town. Even at four in the morning, humans could be heard in the taverns and on the streets. It was only part of what made the town—and the country of Spain in general—so appealing to vampires.

Tucking her into his side, Terry steered the small inflatable away from the larger town and into the black night. They cut across the water, making their way to the safe house tucked into the hills. As soon as Gemma's feet touched land, she breathed deeply, sinking her feet into the rocky soil and drawing deeply from the energy of the earth. It sang beneath her, warming her bones and making her blood rush.

"Hmm." Gemma turned to see Terry blinking a little and looking around. "That's odd."

"Do you feel it?" The energy filled her. She almost felt like laughing, despite the danger they were in. "With my blood, do you feel it?"

Terry shook his head. "I'm sure it's not what you feel, but there's definitely something different."

She reached a hand out and grasped his. "You're warmer, too."

"Am I?" He threw a simple pack over his shoulder and tugged her up the path leading to the rock cottage hidden in the hills. From the outside, it looked like an old, abandoned house, but Gemma had dug into the hills, creating a very comfortable, if small, shelter for them with three secured rooms. When they were in Muros, they sometimes abandoned the parties and meetings to hide there, just for a bit of privacy.

"It feels different," she said shyly. "I imagine this will take some getting used to."

"I imagine so." He moved as confidently over the rocky ground as he did in the water. "Are you glad, Gem?

I'm glad." He abruptly stopped and she almost ran into him. "I'd never imagined you loving me like this. Are you happy? You feel happy. I don't even know how I know that, but—"

Terry stopped when she kissed him. Finally, she pulled away. "Completely unexpected, Terry. Loving you was never the plan. I think that just makes it better, don't you?"

His eyes crinkled in the corners a bit when he smiled. She'd never noticed how attractive that was before. "You and me?" he said. "We won't ever be bored, will we?"

"Never."

CHAPTER NINE

Terry woke that evening with Gemma curled into his side, reading a folder he'd brought from London that detailed their current agreement with Leonor regarding trade in Morocco. He lay still and quiet, appreciating the scene before he began what he knew would be a long night.

There had been a few moments like this in his immortal life, moments he knew at the time were life-altering. Change came slowly when you had hundreds, possibly thousands, of years to live. Change was approached cautiously. With respect. A single turn could alter eternity irrevocably.

But this change...

He had dreamt of it. Fantasized about what it would be if she loved him as he loved her. What it would mean for them both to be true partners? He had no way of predicting how this would change them, but he knew in his heart that it would be for the better.

"You're thinking quite loudly, darling."

"I love that," he said in a voice rough from sleep.

"What?"

"'Darling.' You calling me darling. I love that." He saw her hide her face a bit in the paperwork. "What?"

"I've called you that for years in my mind. I just didn't say it."

He couldn't stop the smile. "Why not?"

She only shrugged, which was fine. He knew how to read her by now. He pulled the manilla folder from her hands and placed it on the small bedside table in the room they now shared.

"Well," he said, "I like it. So feel free to call me that along with the occasional elitist insult, luv."

"I am not an elitist."

He only laughed.

"I'm not! I wasn't born a lady, Terry. Far from it."

"No, you weren't." He ran a hand over her hair. It was still a bit mussed, which pleased him. "You fought and clawed your way where you wanted to be. Made yourself into the person and the vampire you are today."

"I did what had to be done."

"You're extraordinary. It's no wonder I love you."

"And you," she smiled wickedly and threw her leg over him, "have never pretended to be anything but who you are. You say that I'm an elitist, but you're a proud, proud man, Terrance Ramsay."

"I have reason."

"I know," she purred before she leaned down to kiss him. "And I love it. Love that you don't care what anyone else thinks. Love that you make no apologies. You're proud. And I'm proud to be your mate."

Forget the priest. That was better than any vow she could speak. He reached up and grabbed her, pulling her into a fierce embrace. He had to have her that very second.

"Love you." He claimed her mouth with a kiss before he rolled them over, pressing her into the mattress. "So much, Gem."

"I love you, too."

She couldn't say it enough. He reveled in it, moving into her with a satisfied growl. Smiling like a boy as they made love. There was still the barely restrained ferocity between them—they would never be polite lovers—but layering over it was a new tenderness that fed his soul.

She was his. His own. His love. His mate.

Forever.

As she dressed later, he heard her ask, "How are we playing this?"

He was stretched out on the bed. It took her ages to prepare for the night, so he was watching her. She usually dressed in her own rooms, but he was putting an end to that. Watching Gemma was highly entertaining.

Frilly, impractical undergarments that he wanted to take off as soon as she put them on. A loose silk dress that only hinted at her delicate curves. Complicated twists and turns with her hair. Just how many pins did she use? He'd have to pull them all out and count later.

"We play it as it is. We were on our honeymoon and were attacked unexpectedly. Who do you think will be there?"

"I'm vacillating between one of her envoys who was in London—"

"That Guillermo chap?"

"Mmhmm. Either him or someone pulling his strings. There were five sent to us. More than necessary for a simple trade negotiation. I'm wondering if Leonor sent three and whoever orchestrated this sent the rest."

"For what purpose?" He had his own ideas but wanted to know what she was thinking.

"She's being felt out, but by who? Is it someone from outside her organization who's using one of her people? Or is this internal? I suppose we'll find out tonight. Have you called London yet?"

"As soon as we get into town."

"Do you think Leonor knows?"

"About someone trying to cause problems? I'd be shocked if she didn't. She doesn't trust anyone, even her own children."

"It will be interesting to see how she plays this. She knew we were coming?"

"I sent a message when I decided to bring you here. Thought I'd combine a little business with pleasure. Plus, Leonor's always fun for a visit."

"She is. I'm looking forward to spending some time with her after we clear up this unpleasantness."

Terry grinned. Leave it to Gemma to see the big picture. Wipe out enemies at nightfall, then enjoy a drink with friends at midnight. She'd probably try to fit in a bit of shopping if the boutiques hadn't all closed.

By the time he rose, she was putting on a touch of makeup. She didn't need much. She'd been turned quite young and her complexion was a pale cream with just a touch of roses in her cheeks from her bloody feast two nights before.

And his blood.

He hardened just at the thought. He could feel himself in her blood. A new awareness of her, along with the new feelings. It was subtle, a connection that would only grow with years, but it was there. A living, pulsing reminder of her in him, and him in her. Thank God they had eternity. He'd never get enough.

He bent down and nipped at her neck before he began to dress. "Let's get this over with. We have far more pleasurable things to do."

She gave him a smile, fangs long and gleaming in her mouth. "As you wish, my lord."

Forget her careful preparations; he tackled her. "Bloody hell, Gem. We're never going to leave this room if you keep saying things like that."

He could hear their "guest" as soon as he turned onto the road leading to their house. There was only one vampire in the library—a smart move if he wanted Terry and Gemma to hold off attack. Terry heard their housekeeper, Luisa, offering him a drink.

"It's Guillermo," Gemma murmured.

"The ambassador?" Well, Terry grimaced, that explained how they found Carl. "Do you hear anyone else?" Her senses were stronger than his.

"There's another vampire down by the dock. Two behind the house. And... a human sitting in the entry hall."

"That's all?"

"Yes."

Terry nodded. Between him, Gemma, and Luisa, they could easily take care of the threat, but Guillermo would know that, too. Still, he'd come, so he must have wanted to talk. Terry felt Gemma slide her hand in his.

"What night was Leonor expecting us?"

"Probably not till tomorrow, but..."

He didn't need to say it. They were in the Rias. Very little went on unobserved. It was both a threat and a protection. Everyone had spies, which made it nearly impossible to hide, but also very difficult to catch someone by surprise. If Guillermo knew they were there, then Leonor did, too.

Terry and Gemma strode up the front steps of their Spanish home, buzzing through the entry so they came face to face with their guest, who was sipping brandy from a cut crystal glass.

"Buenas noches, Señor y Señora."

"And a good evening to you," Terry said as he sat, pulling Gemma down to his side on the silk-covered chaise. "Luisa, please get Gemma and I our usual drinks."

"Si, Señor Ramsay." Luisa slipped from the room, a tiny figure in an unobtrusive grey dress. She was a fairly young, but terribly efficient, vampire who ran their home in Muros year-round. Luisa's looks were more than deceiving. And so far, she had proven loyal.

"So, Guillermo, how can we help you this evening? You're looking well since we left you in London." Gemma's voice was carefully neutral as Terry sized up his prey. The other vampire looked studiously calm, dressed in a pale linen suit that matched Terry's. It was the standard uniform for immortals vacationing in the Rias.

"I had heard that you sailed into complications while coming from England. I am happy to see you safe in your home, Señora Melcombe."

"Oh?" Gemma was all innocence. "How did you hear of our excitement, Guillermo? Surely only the one who had given out our information would know of the unsuccessful attack."

Terry grinned. No beating around the bush for his

girl.

Guillermo didn't lose a beat. "Unfortunately, I had the information too late to warn you. When I heard of the order from Leonor, I was shocked, naturally. But I was not supposed to know of it. She knew I thought of you and Señor Ramsay as reliable allies for Spain. Wonderful trading partners worthy of closer alliance. It grieved me that Leonor had taken such a step to remove you from power, but I am relieved to know she failed in her attempt. Your loss would be felt through all of Europe. Indeed, the entire immortal world."

"Too true." Terry reached out for the blood wine that Luisa offered him. It was an older batch, but still not unpleasant. He saw Guillermo's eyes widen at the strangely dark port. "If anything were to happen to us, the power vacuum would be felt in far more than just England, wouldn't it?"

Guillermo said, "It is for that reason I have come. To both beg your pardon for my lady's actions and ask for your help. Leonor has become an unreliable ally and leader. There are rumors she has lost control of the Portuguese coast. Her allies in the Spanish court are divided and her power has waned. She is obviously becoming rash to make decisions such as the one to attack you and your lovely wife."

Idiot. Could he have been more obvious? Guillermo was definitely not working for Leonor. So who...

"It's horrible," Gemma said, "to be faced with these dilemmas. To be forced to part allegiance with those you thought you could trust."

"Sad indeed." Terry patted Gemma's knee as he caught Luisa's eye. She was moving toward the door of the library. "But a choice between your own survival and that of someone you once considered a friend is really no choice at all."

"Survival," Guillermo said, his fangs dropping a little, "must always come first. Do I have your support, Señor Ramsay?"

"Let's not be hasty." He sipped his blood wine and linked his fingers with Gemma's. "I need to know what your current situation is, Guillermo."

"I have no desire to remain under the aegis of a waning leader," he said. "I have been cultivating my own allies for some time."

Well, isn't that interesting?

"Is that so?" Gemma latched onto his statement. "So were those your allies in England with you? Or Leonor's?"

"I may have suggested a few additions to the initial trade party," Guillermo said with a twisted smile. "Leonor was happy to hear my suggestions."

"Surely a sign of her growing weakness," Gemma added with a look of regret. "To not realize how such a large trade party would be viewed."

Terry said, "We were suspicious as soon as we met you."

"I had hoped to put you on your guard."

Terry grinned. "I just bet you did."

Guillermo cocked his head. "To warn you, of course. I hoped to cultivate an alliance between us. I knew Leonor did not value your relationship as she should. And then I heard of the ordered attack on the Conquest. After knowing that she would send others to kill you in such a manner... I simply cannot, in good conscience, remain at her side."

"So you're coming to us for protection?"

"I'm coming to offer you an alternative."

And now we get to the heart of it. Terry took another sip of wine. Stale. Yes, the newer batch was much better. "Do tell, Guillermo. What kind of alternative could you offer my wife and I? Yourself? How many allies do you bring with you? You're a trade envoy. A second lieutenant, if my information is correct."

"It is not only myself that I bring. I do have allies of my own, Señor Ramsay."

He leaned back in the chaise, the picture of relaxation as Gemma lounged against him. "What kind of allies?"

"Those who think ahead. Who look to the future. Too long have our kind been in the shadows, Señor. We are the gods of old. We should be kings over humanity, not hiding away, content to play by their rules."

"Why should we have much to do with them at all?" Gemma asked. "They're our food source. We have little to do with them unless we must."

Terry tried not to snort when he imagined the look on Wilhelmina's face if she heard Gemma just then. He imagined the secretary would stake her employer herself.

"The human world encroaches into our own more every decade. Technology will force us to deal with them eventually. My allies are those who wish to harness humans and put them in their rightful place. Why should we be the ones hiding?"

It was the same imperialistic mumbo-jumbo his sire warned him about two hundred years before. Terry tried not to sigh. There would always be those of their kind who saw humans, not as a related species, but as an inferior one. It was hard not to, at times. But Terry was young enough to remember what it had been to be human, and he purposefully kept close enough to mortals to remind himself. So did Gemma, whether she realized it or not.

Those of their kind who remained mixed with the mortal world were better survivors. More adaptable. They could function and hide and prosper in ways the more segregated could not. Further, humanity was growing stronger every day. To him, that meant adaptation. Evolution. To others? It meant biting back. Annoying, really.

"My allies foresee a time when humanity is ruled by us, as they should be. Then we will control them and their technology, not the other way round. As I said, they think ahead."

"It sounds as if they think backward, if you'd ask my opinion."

Guillermo's eyes flashed. "If that is your opinion, Señor—"

"It is both our opinion," Gemma said. "Do you think us so fickle that we would part ways with an ally who has remained in favor for far longer than you have lived?"

"She ordered an attack on you. She does not trust you." Amnis crackled in the room as the water vampire began to lose control.

"No, she didn't." Terry set down his drink. "You did."

"I did no such—"

"Maybe if you appreciated the human's technology a bit more, you'd realize we've already been on the phone to London, Guillermo." Terry stood as the other vampire jumped to his feet. "Maybe you'd realize that my head of security has already investigated the death of Carl Stanton. Maybe you'd realize he kept records of your meeting in his electronic organizer."

Guillermo bared his fangs and started toward the door, only to be halted by the tiny form of Luisa, who stood in front of it, a bloody dagger in her hand and fangs bared.

"Luisa, have the others been dispatched?" Gemma asked.

"Si, Señora." She brought the blade up and licked at a drop of blood. "I left the human alive for later."

"He may have nothing to do with Guillermo's betrayal. We'll question him, but leave his fate to Leonor," Terry added.

The Spaniard stood frozen in the middle of the room. "Leonor will hear of this. You have started a war."

Terry roared in laughter. "You can't have it both ways, boy! Do you think she'll believe your word over ours? With what has happened here tonight?"

Guillermo sneered. "You know nothing. Do you know who I—"

"Who you are?" Gemma broke in. "Of course we do. I only grieve that my old friend has to face the decision you have forced on her. I hear her coming right now, in fact."

The look of horror on the vampire's face could not be hidden. His eyes darted around the room, but Terry only said quietly, "Try it. Luisa is very quick with the knife, you know. She used to perform on stage."

The round-faced immortal beamed from the doorway as Guillermo shifted his eyes toward the windows. Luisa edged closer as Terry felt Leonor's energy approaching.

"Luisa," Gemma said, "would you be so kind as to greet our guest and her entourage at the door? Please see if they'd like any refreshment."

Luisa bowed slightly and backed away. Guillermo started to edge toward the door again.

"Do try," Gemma said, at his side in the blink of an eye. "Killing you would be worth ruining this dress."

Terry saw Guillermo trying to muster his courage. "When Leonor—"

"When I what?" The Spanish noblewoman entered the room with not even a whisper. She leaned against the wall and edged the library door closed with the tip of one designer heel. Gemma backed away. "When I arrive? Do finish your sentence, Guillermo, for I am here."

"Leonor," Terry said. "Welcome. Has Luisa taken care of you?"

The stunning woman raised a single eyebrow. "Luisa has taken care of quite a lot this evening, including me."

Gemma stood to greet the Spanish leader. "Leonor. How are you?"

"I am sad, my friend. How true it is: To be forced to part allegiance with those you thought you could trust is sad, indeed."

Guillermo lurched toward her. "*Madre*—"

In a blur, she had him by the throat, fangs bared and wine-colored nails cutting into her child's neck. "Do not call me your mother," she spat in Spanish. "Did you think I would not know of your trifling attempts? I am only sorry that my friends were pulled into this. You have shamed me. Shamed my court with your petty manipulations and delusions of grandeur."

"*Madre*—Leonor... I can explain." Guillermo forced out in a strangled voice.

"No, you cannot." She lifted him higher. "I will extract every piece of information about these allies of yours. Then, my son, I will kill you."

"You wouldn't." Guillermo's voice came in a high desperate whine.

Leonor's voice was tinged with sorrow. "You know I will."

A crashing sound came from the hall, a shattering of glass, then suddenly, the room was filled with smoke.

"Tear gas!" Gemma yelled.

"Smoke grenades, too." Terry snarled as the cloud filled the room. The gas did little to affect vampire breathing as they didn't need oxygen, but it did cause the eyes to water and the scent was overwhelming to his sensitive nose. He heard Leonor hiss and drop Guillermo, but could see nothing as the grey smoke began to fill the room.

"Gemma?" he shouted.

"Luisa?" He heard her calling for the maid and bodyguard. "Luisa, where are you?"

A flurry of voices yelled in Spanish, some he recognized, some he did not. Terry's only thought was for Gemma. Just as he was about to burst into a rage, he felt her grab his hand. The blood leapt in his veins as she pulled him closer.

"They've broken into the house," she said. "I can't see or hear—"

Just then, a frustrated scream rose from the clouded room and the sound of windows shattering broke through the confusion. Terry lunged toward the voice.

"Leonor!"

More glass shattered as vampires poured into the room. Terry recognized the small form of their housekeeper as she methodically went to each window, breaking it and clearing the room of smoke.

"Leonor?" Gemma shouted.

"I'm here." Her voice was hoarse, but she was surrounded by four vampires dressed in dark grey suits. There was no Guillermo in sight. "Damn my arrogance. I should have brought my guard."

"You had no way of knowing, my lady," one murmured as he held out a handkerchief.

Terry looked back at Gemma, but his wife was already composing herself, dabbing at blood-tinged tears that stained her face and ordering Luisa to bring wine for their guests. Terry swiped at his face, brushing back the helping hands of their humans, who had come from the servants quarters upstairs.

Leonor coughed once more, then pushed away from her guards, stalking toward Terry. "What was that?"

"That was a very smart attack, Leonor. Whoever grabbed your child did not want him talking about what he knew."

Gemma handed him a warm towel to wipe his face. "I heard no vampires approach. Did you?"

"No. All I felt was the normal human activity on the street."

Leonor's guard added, "And I sensed no danger from the boat until I heard you yell, my lady."

"They used humans?" Leonor gaped. "Is it possible?"

"Smart, in a way," Gemma said. "We usually don't

consider them as threats. And armed with the tear gas..."

"It was a well-planned attack." Terry shrugged off the humans who were trying to be helpful and directed them to clean up the broken glass. "They didn't try to attack any of us. They knew they'd lose. It was a grab. Surprise us. Throw the gas canisters. Grab Guillermo. He probably went willingly, thinking it was a rescue."

Leonor's face was grim. "I don't imagine it was."

"I agree," Gemma said. "I very much doubt we will see your youngest again, Lea. I am so sorry."

The flash of grief in her eyes was the only indication Terry saw of her loss. "He signed his own death warrant when he chose to work against me. I am only sorry I could not get more information from him. I am grateful for your loyalty, Gemma. And yours, Terrance. This will not be forgotten. Please excuse this horrid attack on your home. The repairs are my responsibility, of course."

As Gemma and Leonor started on the polite noises of hostess and guest, Terry surveyed the room. The Spanish guards hovered around Gemma and their leader; Luisa directed the humans in the clean up of the glass and clearing the rooms. Fans were brought in, but quickly taken away when one of Leonor's guards was revealed as a wind vampire.

Terry stood at the broken window, staring into the lights of the harbor that twinkled as live music drifted in from the bars and clubs in town. Just then, he saw a large yacht moving away from the dock, a lone figure standing on the deck, looking back at him.

"Gemma," he called, and his mate rushed to his side.

"What is it, darling?"

He blinked, trying to see more of the boat, but the

moon was only a sliver in the sky, and the pale grey silhouette was already obscured by the mist. "Not sure. Might be nothing. Is everyone well?"

"Other than annoyed, Leonor is fine. It was obviously not an attack, only an extraction. Guillermo was being watched."

"Apparently. He won't be alive for long."

"No, I doubt he will."

He felt her energy slide along his a moment before she knit their fingers together. "Are you sure you're all right? What were you looking at?"

He shrugged. "Probably nothing."

Gemma cocked an eyebrow. "Possibly something?"

He smiled. "We'll see, won't we?"

"Whatever it is, I doubt we'll be bored."

"With you?" Terry threw an arm around her shoulder. "I can't even imagine."

EPILOGUE

Gemma found him in the large workshop in the Temple. It used to contain his sire's old holding cells and interrogation rooms, but Terry had turned it into storage and workspace, maintaining the old water channels that led to the river.

"Terry?"

She heard the rasping sound as she entered the stairwell. His amnis reached out, touching hers for a moment, before beckoning her farther underground. She followed the sound to see him working on the shell of his new sailboat. His shirt was stripped off and he wore only a pair of work pants as he methodically planed and sanded the wood at human speed.

Gemma could tell he was thinking. Though it didn't tire him, the routine of physical exertion was one way Terry had always chosen to quiet his thoughts so he could make sense of the jumble of information his immortal brain processed. Some vampires played chess. Gemma still rode horses. Terry built boats.

He paused and glanced up, beckoning her over with a finger. In the background, she could hear the water lapping in the underground canal.

Terry didn't say a word, just took her hand and ran her fingers along the board he'd been sanding at the workbench. His amnis wrapped up her arm as she touched the soft wood, a tingle spreading from her fingertips, up the inside of her wrist, and over her shoulder until Terry's energy was followed by the soft feel of his lips on the inside of her elbow.

"What—"

"Shhh," he whispered, then he was leaning into her neck, a hint of stubble scraping against her collarbone as he kissed her.

Since Spain, he had become even more expressive in his affection, knowing instinctually how much she craved it. It was far more than the physical relationship they had shared before. He had become as much a part of Gemma as her own limbs.

He held her there, one hand resting on her waist, the other holding her cheek gently as he leisurely enjoyed her mouth. After a few moments, he pulled away, smiling.

"Hello, luv."

"Miss me?" He'd seen her at nightfall when he woke.

"Always." Terry looked down. "Sorry. Got your dress a bit dusty."

Gemma only shrugged and looked over at the new project. "It's looking more like a boat every week."

"That's the goal now, isn't it?" He grinned. "What are you busy with tonight?"

"I finished going over the inventory and expenditures for the shelters with Mina. She's taken a liking to Bernard, by the way."

Terry grunted when she mentioned his new human secretary. Gemma imagined he still missed Carl. It was taking a while to warm up to the new man, no matter how efficient he was.

"And I've cleared up the details on the trade meeting with Ernesto's people."

"Will Baojia be there?"

"I think he's still in San Diego."

Terry growled. He and Don Ernesto Alvarez had a good working relationship, but it had been tested by Ernesto's treatment of his head of security, who Terry considered a friend. The immortal leader of Southern California could be a hard man, and one known to hold a grudge.

"Don't let it become a wedge, darling. He's an important ally."

"I know that. But he's being a fool over sentiment."

According to rumor, Baojia had let a favored relative of Ernesto's come to harm. Gemma knew it to be the father of Beatrice De Novo, Ernesto's favorite granddaughter. Since then, the skilled water vampire had been exiled to minor assignments in San Diego and out of active participation in Ernesto's business and political negotiations.

"What did you want to talk about?" Gemma asked. He'd sent a note with Roger for her to join him when he usually liked working alone.

"I've been thinking about Spain again." He stepped back and picked up the wood plane, going to work on another plank that would form part of the bow. "Can't seem to get it off my mind."

"Neither can I," she said with a satisfied smile.

He laughed. "Not the fun part, the other bit."

"Oh?" She sat in a scarred chair next to the workbench and watched him get back to work.

"Leonor in Spain." He ran the plane down the board

with a level thrust.

"Who appears to be stabilizing her position since she rid herself of Guillermo."

"Mmhmm. Murphy in Dublin." He took another long swipe and a curl of wood fell to the floor.

"Also seems stabilized now, particularly with Carwyn and Brigid nearby."

"Jean Desmarais in Marseilles. The Dutchmen your brother spoke about." He planed the board again. "Me."

She nodded, starting to see his train of thought. "All facing challenges or unforeseen threats in the last year or so."

"Just when we start hearing more rumors about this bloody Elixir drug."

"What are you thinking?"

He paused, hand resting on the board. "What do they all have in common, Gem?"

She blinked. It was so obvious. Why hadn't she realized it before? "Shipping."

Terry nodded. "Shipping."

"All those being felt out by whoever was pulling Guillermo's strings have strong shipping interests." Of course! Gemma wanted to kick herself for not seeing it sooner.

"You always were a brilliant woman."

"A bit slow on this one. Have you talked to my father?"

"Not yet. I want to meet with Ernesto first. All the major Atlantic shipping powers are being felt out for weaknesses. I'm curious about the Pacific. The Dutch still go back and forth; we might try a meeting with them if your brother could arrange something."

"He will. If nothing else than to repay the favor for Rene. I haven't heard anything from the Scandinavians, but then, they tend to be very close-lipped."

"See if Jetta is amenable to a meeting. I believe she sired that bloke who attacked Brigid. You could feel out her position."

"So whoever is behind the Elixir manufacturing is involved in shipping."

Terry nodded. "Either involved or wants to be." He swept the wood plane down the board once more before he paused. "Hundreds... thousands of years, luv. Some things don't change much. You control the oceans..."

"You command trade. Especially in our world."

"The richest immortals are still those who rule the seas, Gem. God knows that's how we've made our fortune."

She stood. "So, what do we do?"

Terry shrugged. "Keep an eye on the water and fortify our position. Keep in touch with allies like Alvarez and Murphy. That's all we can do right now." He set down the tool and walked toward her. "We'll be fine. We just have to be careful. But you and I..." He put an arm around her waist and pulled her hard against him, swooping down to place a searing kiss on her mouth. "We're a force to be reckoned with. I'm not worried about us."

Gemma purred in pleasure, tucking her hands under his waistband and against the cool silk of his skin. "Did you really only ask me here to talk politics and strategy?"

"No." Terry grinned and tossed her over his shoulder. "We've got a boat to christen, don't we?"

THE END

Dear readers,

This little story had an unusual start. I love Terry and Gemma. I've loved them since they first appeared in *This Same Earth*, but I didn't really know whether they had enough of a story to warrant a whole novel. I knew they had a different kind of relationship, and didn't really know how Elemental Mystery and Elemental World readers would like it, to be honest.

Toward the end of 2012, I was coming to the end of a very hard year. I decided I wanted to finally write Terry and Gemma's love story, even though it wasn't a full book. Even though it was just for fun.

Because really, it was just for me. I needed to take a deep breath and connect with readers more directly. I needed the pure fun of writing again. I decided to post *Waterlocked* on my website as free fiction for my dedicated readers, and see if they might enjoy it, too.

I wrote. I sent it to my most excellent first reader, Kristine M. Todd. Then I posted. I posted one chapter a week, and I was *overwhelmed* by the reaction. I had the highest site traffic in my blog's history on posting days! Needless to say, it was incredibly gratifying to read the comments from my wonderful fans who enjoyed a lighter love story like *Waterlocked*.

It was just what I needed.

I finished up the editing on the first Cambio Springs book, *Shifting Dreams,* and started on the next full novel in the Elemental World series, *Blood and Sand.* I finished the first draft in record time, just over two months, and the story will be published this summer.

Thank you to everyone who enjoyed Gemma and Terry along with me. And thank you to readers who are reading it in its final form, too. I hope you enjoyed reading it as much as I enjoyed writing it.

Thanks for reading,
Elizabeth

ELIZABETH HUNTER is a contemporary fantasy, paranormal romance, and paranormal mystery writer. She is a graduate of the University of Houston Honors College and a former English teacher. She once substitute taught a kindergarten class but decided that middle school was far less frightening. Thankfully, people now pay her to write books and eighth graders everywhere rejoice.

She currently lives in Central California with her son, two dogs, many plants, and a sadly empty fish tank. She is the author of the Elemental Mysteries and Elemental World series, the Cambio Springs series, the Irin Chronicles, and other works of fiction.

ALSO BY ELIZABETH HUNTER

The Irin Chronicles

The Scribe
The Singer
The Secret
On a Clear Winter Night (short story)
The Staff and the Blade
The Silent

The Cambio Springs Series

Shifting Dreams
Long Ride Home (short story)
Desert Bound
Five Mornings (short story)
Waking Hearts

Contemporary Romance

The Genius and the Muse

Made in the USA
Monee, IL
23 January 2020

20732131R00083